"Do you think you can walk in here and take over my life, just like that?"

Kyle shrugged casually. "Probably not. But it would be nice," he added, almost as an afterthought. His hands moved to her arms, holding her gently but firmly. "Let's face it, Angie. That contest is important. I have a feeling we may get more out of it than we bargained for."

Now that she was this close to him, Angie's heart began beating at an alarming rate. She wondered nervously if he was aware of her galloping pulse. His head bent to gaze directly into her eyes, and his hands tightened intimately on her arms.

"Admit it," he said huskily. "You want to do it."

"Do what?" she whispered breathlessly, and in that one unfortunate double entendre, she knew she was lost. A sly twinkle stole into his eyes, and the inches between them disappeared.

"You'd better stop me now, Angie," he murmured, his lips against hers, "or you won't be able to stop me at all."

Diana Morgan *is a pseudonym for a husband-and-wife team. They met at a phone booth at Columbia University, and have been together romantically and professionally ever since. They enjoy opera, pigging out, small children and elves (especially their daughter Elizabeth), their retreat in the Berkshires, and trying to figure out what will happen next on Hill Street Blues.*

Dear Reader:

Summer may be ending, but this month's SECOND CHANCE AT LOVE romances will keep the fun alive. We begin with...

Anything Goes (#286) by Diana Morgan. This is the fifteenth romance—but a first for SECOND CHANCE AT LOVE—by this husband-and-wife writing team. And what a zany romp it is! Angie Carpenter, who's just been named Supermom by a national magazine, becomes so incensed by wily inventor Kyle Bennett that she vows to uphold housewives and the American way by beating Kyle's six-armed robot in a televised contest. But she doesn't reckon on falling in love with Kyle! *Anything Goes* boasts what must be one of the most original reasons for interrupting a love scene—Benny the robot arrives unexpectedly to serve lunch! Angie's mortified. You, on the other hand, may never stop laughing.

Poisoned peanut butter may sound like a "sticky" basis for a romance, but in *Sophisticated Lady* (#287) Elissa Curry adds a mouth-watering hero and a never-stuck-up heroine to create a delicious love story. The problem is that Mick Piper's being accused of poisoning his *own* peanut butter (he manufactures the stuff), and Abigail Vanderbine, who's come to interview him and ends up staying, is determined to find out who's really responsible. You'll find Elissa's magic touch in the gleefully witty repartee and oh, so sexy situations. And be sure not to miss the cameo appearance by Grace and Luke Lazurnovich from Elissa's *Lady Be Good* (#247)!

In *The Phoenix Heart* (#288) by Betsy Osborne, proper Bostonian Alyssa Courtney is sure she'll never adjust to laid-back, freaked-out California—especially once she meets gulpingly handsome cartoonist Rade Stone. Suddenly she's living in a state of constant crisis, and falling in love with a man whom her job requires she expose as an evil influence on children! Even her kids turn traitors by being on their worst behavior around Rade. Don't miss this tenderly warm romance filled with laughter and loving.

In *Fallen Angel* (#289), Carole Buck creates a powerfully emotional love story. Beautiful, vulnerable Mallory Victor is caught between two worlds: the upper-crust New England world of hero Dr. David Hitchcock, and the glittery but ultimately shallow world of rock music—where, unknown to David, she induces hysteria in teen-aged fans as rock's "bad girl," Molly V. Using both Mallory's and David's points of view to very skillful effect, Carole deeply involves us in these two characters' dilemma. Carole says *she* cried as she wrote the last thirty pages. Maybe you'd better keep some tissues handy, just in case...

Hilary Cole adds a fresh voice to romances in *The Sweetheart Trust* (#290). Here, the desirous thoughts of two mystery writers put zing into their literary collaboration. Kate Fairchild has already fallen hard for impossibly charming, delightfully unpredictable, infuriatingly witty Nick Trent. When she inherits a decrepit Victorian mansion, she seizes the opportunity to domesticate Nick in a country setting. But rural life includes unexpected—often hilarious—complications ... and none of the guarantees Kate's looking for. Lots of you raved about Hilary Cole's TO HAVE AND TO HOLD romance, *My Darling Detective* (#34). You'll be even more enchanted by *The Sweetheart Trust*.

Finally, in *Dear Heart* (#291) we bring you a delightful new tale from an old favorite, Lee Williams. Why does Charly Lynn gravitate toward children and lovingly nurture the animals in the pet store she helps run? Bret Roberts doesn't have time to find out. He's too busy stealing kisses ... and trying to survive the antics of a hysterical monkey in little red pants who decides to take someone's car for a joy ride on a San Francisco hill! The fact that Bret is allergic to animals—and Charly houses innumerable dogs, cats, a rabbit, and a parakeet in her small apartment—complicates the rocky romance between this hapless couple, who are otherwise perfect for each other. Or almost... When things get really rough, Charly writes to "Dear Mr. Heart," the local advice columnist, begging for help ... never realizing what further trouble she's getting into!

Enjoy! Warm wishes,

Ellen Edwards

Ellen Edwards, Senior Editor
SECOND CHANCE AT LOVE
The Berkley Publishing Group
200 Madison Avenue
New York, NY 10016

ANYTHING GOES

DIANA MORGAN

SECOND CHANCE AT LOVE BOOK

ANYTHING GOES

Copyright © 1985 by Irene Goodman and Alex Kamaroff

All rights reserved. No part of this publication may be reproduced or transmitted in any form or by any means, electronic or mechanical, including photocopy, recording, or any information storage and retrieval system, without permission in writing from the publisher.

Requests for permission to make copies of any part of the work should be mailed to: Permissions, Second Chance at Love, The Berkley Publishing Group, 200 Madison Avenue, New York, NY 10016.

First edition published September 1985

First printing

"Second Chance at Love" and the butterfly emblem are trademarks belonging to Jove Publications, Inc.

Printed in the United States of America

Second Chance at Love books are published by
The Berkley Publishing Group
200 Madison Avenue, New York, NY 10016

To Gabrielle Katz, Superkid

ANYTHING GOES

MODERN WOMAN MAGAZINE'S
SUPERMOM CONTEST

Tell us why your mom is a Supermom in twenty-five words or less:

1) She's a sweetheart
2) She is like a doctor
3) when you have a night mayer she comforts you
4) She Teachs you like any Other teacher.
5) she's eclectic.

Name: Samantha Carpeater Age: 9
Address: 3312 Clark Rd.
City: Smithtown State: Ny Zip: 11582

Contest expires November 30. All decisions of the judges are final. Children of employees of Modern Woman, Inc., not eligible.

Chapter One

"THIS LITTLE FELLOW is going to put the American housewife out of business."

Angie Carpenter whipped around to stare at the TV monitors in her dressing room. On camera one she could see the striking, energetic man who had made that outrageous statement, and the second screen was focusing on a close-up of the "little fellow." He was a three-foot-high cylinder with six spiderlike mechanical arms and a twirling headpiece that flashed red and white lights.

Angie's nine-year-old daughter looked at the screen and laughed. "Looks like R2-D2, huh, Mom?" she said, her chestnut braids swinging as she swiveled back to her mother.

Angie chuckled indulgently, her husky laugh disguising her vague annoyance. "If it can fold contour sheets, I'll buy one."

A harried young man holding a clipboard stuck his head inside the dressing room. "You're on in eight minutes, Supermom."

He disappeared as abruptly as he had come, and Angie sighed. "I wish he wouldn't call me that."

"But it's your title, Mom," Samantha insisted, her large brown eyes growing wider. "You earned it."

"I know, sweetheart. Well, here we go. How do I look?" Angie smoothed her crisp white suit into place and patted her wavy, chin-length blond hair. She had a wholesome, womanly look that didn't quite conceal the tigerish sensuality underneath. Her hazel eyes were candid and disarming, but when she smiled, there was a sudden hint of smoke.

"Copacetic, Mom. Really pulchritudinous."

This time Angie had to laugh. Samantha seemed determined to outclass every other kid in the fourth grade with the use of a dictionary calendar her father had sent her. Each day on the calendar listed a new word, as well as the definition and the use of the word in a sample sentence. Today was June third, one hundred and fifty-four days into the year, and Samantha had learned one hundred and fifty-four new words, few of which Angie knew the meaning of.

"Women are no longer useful in the home," the current guest on the show was saying casually, as if this preposterous statement could be accepted as fact by any intelligent person. His lake-blue eyes sparkled as he said this, and Angie mindlessly registered the fact that he was devastatingly attractive before she promptly dismissed it as quite irrelevant.

"Who is this clown, anyway?" she muttered aloud.

The paunchy, nattily dressed host of the show, Biff

Anything Goes 3

Marvin, unwittingly answered her question. "We're speaking with Mr. Kyle Bennett, who has just invented the ultimate gadget that will get the little woman out of the house—permanently."

"Oh, brother!" Angie snorted. "And I have to go on after that?"

She continued to watch as the robot was put through a demonstration of its skills. A vacuum cleaner had been set up on stage next to an ironing board, and as Angie looked on in surprise, the inventor gave it orders.

"Vacuum! Go!" he said, stressing both words.

The robot suddenly perked up, its lights flashing, and after a few seconds of emitting tabulation sounds like a cash register, it made its way across the floor on its tractor wheels. The audience reacted with surprise that turned to awe and finally amusement as the thing picked up the vacuum hose with a mechanical arm and proceeded to clean the stage.

"Benny responds to fifteen verbal commands," the inventor explained, evidently happily aware that the audience was in the palm of his hand.

"Benny?" Angie laughed in disbelief. "He calls that thing Benny?"

"Now watch this." Like a true showman, Kyle Bennett paused to heighten the effect. "Benny!" he called out. "Vacuum! Iron! Both go!"

To the astonishment of everyone, the robot now extended three more mechanical arms and began to iron a pair of pants on the ironing board. One hand continued to vacuum as another ironed, while the third and fourth hands held the pants and a can of spray starch.

The audience reacted with a mixture of surprise and delight, bursting into scattered applause. "Six hands are better than two," Biff quipped as he walked over to stand beside the robot.

"I wonder if it can do my homework!" Samantha piped up. She turned to her mother for confirmation, but Angie was wearing a slight frown.

"Why do I have the feeling I'm being set up?" she muttered to herself. "Supermom versus the Six-Handed Wonder from Outer Space."

The inventor was sauntering over to the host. "Put Benny up against the toughest competition," he said confidently, "and they'll throw down their mops and brooms and surrender."

"No more ring around the collar," Biff joked.

"Say good-bye to waxy yellow buildup," Kyle added.

The two men laughed together, but Angie compressed her lips in annoyance. "Listen to those two idiots," she fumed. "They actually believe that garbage."

"Would you like your jacket brushed?" Benny's creator asked the host. Before Biff could answer, more commands followed. "Benny, stop all!" Kyle ordered, again punching the words with his voice. The iron and vacuum were instantly disengaged. "Groom! Go!"

The robot changed direction and headed for the host, who instinctively backed off a little. "I hope he doesn't mistake me for Darth Vader," he said to the camera, earning a modest laugh.

Suddenly, all six of the robot's arms extended and began working on the host's sports jacket, removing lint and brushing it down. "The ultimate butler," Biff said in wonder. The audience laughed and applauded as Benny went through his paces. "Now if only I can get my wife to do this," he cracked. But the women in the audience, obviously outnumbering the men, booed his last remark.

Anything Goes

He looked at them and shrank back a little. "I think my wife is going to kill me for that last statement."

"Does she ever ask you to take out the garbage?" Kyle asked him.

Biff shrugged. "All the time. Why?"

"Watch this." With a confident smirk, Kyle ordered, "Benny! Garbage!"

The robot trundled over to the host's desk and immediately picked up the wastepaper basket. He carried it neatly offstage to the applause of the entire audience.

"And they say you can't get good help nowadays," Biff boomed jovially. He turned to the middle camera. "And we'll be back in just a few minutes with our next guest, the winner of *Modern Woman* magazine's Supermom contest." He winked. "I'm curious to see what she'll have to say about our friend Benny here."

"Benny!" Angie snapped. "Who said anything about that overgrown tin can? It's that creep of an inventor I'd like to get my hands on."

"Careful, Mom," Samantha warned. "Don't let him start something."

"Four minutes, Mrs. Carpenter."

Angie took a deep breath and prepared to do battle. In a very short time, millions of eyes would be watching her every move over their morning coffee.

"Ready to face the music?" she asked her daughter.

It was a rhetorical question. There was very little that fazed the eminently pragmatic Samantha. The nine-year-old jumped off her stool, and together she and Angie followed the young man through an array of cables and ladders until they were standing behind a curtain right next to the host's desk. Angie peeked through it for a second to steal a look at the audience. She caught a glimpse of flashing smiles and expectant faces and swallowed hard. Off to her right sat the toupeed Biff Marvin and the good-looking inventor, who had already moved over to make room for her and Samantha.

"Fifteen seconds!" someone called out.

Angie stood up straight and took a long, slow breath. As she waited anxiously, she suddenly felt a persistent tugging at her skirt.

"What is it, Samantha?" she hissed under her breath.

"What's what, Mom?"

"Ten seconds! Places, everyone!"

The tugging continued, and Angie twisted around to look questioningly at her daughter, who smiled innocently.

"Five seconds—"

She could hear the shuffling of chairs and a scratchy sound as the host adjusted his microphone. "Which camera, Harry?" he asked.

"Four, three, two—"

The tugging hadn't stopped, and Angie's nerves jumped. "Not now, Samantha," she snapped.

"We're back again," Biff Marvin was saying smoothly into the camera. "Our next guest is a mother, but she's a very unusual mother. She's a Supermom."

Still annoyed by the tugging, Angie looked down, expecting to see her daughter's hand. Instead, she saw a spidery mechanical arm pulling at her dress.

"Would you please welcome Mrs. Angie Carpenter and her daughter, Samantha."

"Cue music," they heard a voice say, and the strains of an upbeat, lively tune began to sound in the studio. "Let's go, Mom," Samantha said.

"I can't," Angie answered frantically. "This thing won't let me go."

The host looked expectantly over to the curtain where Samantha was busily trying to disengage the robot from her mother's skirt, but it wouldn't release her.

"Maybe if I give it one swift kick," Angie said, threatening the thing with her right foot.

"No, no!" It was the inventor's voice. He ran directly in front of the camera to join them, momentarily upsetting Biff Marvin's flawless composure. The music died down abruptly, letting the words reach the microphones loud and clear. "Whatever you do," he pleaded, "don't get rough. Please be gentle with him." He gazed into her eyes with an engaging look of supplication that Angie found disturbing, and she quickly looked away.

Perceiving what was going on now, the audience began to laugh and buzz with speculation, and Biff, after throwing an isn't-this-hilarious look at the camera, got up and joined the struggling group at the curtain. Angie looked up and saw the merciless eye of the camera staring at her flushed face. She tried gamely to smile, but inside she was growing more and more agitated.

"Well, well," Biff said heartily. "It seems this little fellow knows his competition."

"Ugh," Angie sputtered. "I'd like to take a can opener to this thing."

"Benny!" the inventor barked. "Clamp off!"

The metal claws suddenly opened, and Angie was free.

"He was just taking lint from your dress," Kyle Bennett explained with disarming earnestness. "He's programmed for grooming as well as shining shoes, and—"

"But he—he attacked me!" Angie exclaimed, trying to retain her composure in front of the camera.

"Benny? Attack?" Kyle looked down affectionately at

the robot and actually patted its metal head. "Down, boy! Heel!" The robot drew in its arms and waited motionlessly. "Man's best friend," Kyle remarked, flashing Angie a dazzling smile.

She gave him a withering glance. "I think you've got a screw loose." She pointed down at Benny. "And I'd like to loosen a few of *his* screws as well."

"That's not nice," he answered, bristling with indignation. "You don't have to take your frustrations and feelings of inadequacy out on this poor, defenseless machine."

"What?!" Angie almost choked. "If you can't keep your contraption under control, I can hardly be responsible—"

"Now, now," Biff broke in, trying to regain control of his show. "It seems we're starting off on the wrong foot here. Why don't we all just begin again?"

"Fine with me," the inventor responded smoothly. "Benny!" he said. "Make up with the lady." And again punching his words, he gave another command. "Shake hands!"

To everyone's amazement, the robot blinked a few lights and extended one of its metal arms. Angie had no choice but to take the arm gingerly and move it up and down. The audience, clearly enjoying every bit of this impromptu exchange, broke into delighted laughter, and Biff Marvin took advantage of the mood. "Shall we sit down and introduce ourselves?" he suggested, gesturing politely toward the desk.

The robot made a sudden, high-pitched beep and then darted over to the couches, where it stopped and retracted its arms, waiting patiently for everyone to join it. The audience laughed again and then broke into spontaneous applause. Angie mustered a weak smile. She knew she had to look like a good sport, but the robot had already upstaged her and had stolen valuable seconds from her allotted on-camera time.

"Don't worry," Kyle assured her silkily. "Benny's beep is worse than his bite."

"I hope so," she answered evenly.

They all arranged themselves on the sofa, Samantha sitting between her mother and Kyle Bennett, and the host taking his usual seat behind the desk. Benny remained stationed next to them, his lights blinking mysteriously.

"I think he's cute," Samantha whispered too loudly.

"If you like metal monsters," Angie muttered back.

"I wasn't talking about the robot, Mom."

Angie almost missed a beat, but then she replied, "Neither was I."

Kyle candidly overheard this conversation and gave Angie another dazzling smile. She wanted to turn away and direct her attention to the host, but something in the man's clear blue eyes stopped her. She hadn't really had a good look at him before; she had been too busy railing against him. But now that she was gazing at him up close, she saw that his lean, irregular face was marked with a keen intelligence and a sense of private determination.

His features were not classic—they were too original for that—but they had a strength and clarity of their own. Most striking of all were his eyes. A brilliant shade of blue, they seemed to miss nothing, and he had the uncanny ability to challenge her without saying a word. Angie hadn't come here to be challenged, but there was something about his bold scrutiny of her that made her want to force him to eat his words. His long, lean body seemed to be filled with restless energy, even though he was lounging carelessly on the couch. The blue eyes crinkled slightly as if reading her thoughts, and suddenly the air was charged with electricity.

"Are we all settled?" Biff asked, oblivious to the current that was running between his two guests. "Good." He turned to face the audience and addressed them with practiced ease. "About a year ago, Samantha Carpenter secretly entered her mother in *Modern Woman*'s Supermom contest. She stated, in twenty-five words or less, why she thinks her mom is a Supermom. Hers was one of hundreds of thousands of entries, and it won first prize." Beaming, he turned to Samantha. "Tell us, Samantha, what exactly is a Supermom?"

Samantha was ready with her answer. "A Supermom is a mom who can do just about anything," she announced. "It's not only being a good mom, it's knowing how to take care of the house, and have a job, and—and just be really swell," she finished in a rush.

Angie smiled graciously at these words of praise, but out of the corner of her eye she saw Kyle Bennett's eyebrow arch suddenly.

"The modern woman, eh?" Biff nodded. "Tell us about your job, Mrs. Carpenter."

Angie smiled and spoke up in her sweet but husky voice. "I write a helpful hints column for the *Long Island Eagle*. But since I won this contest, my column's been picked up by a number of other papers. I spend about four hours a day at the office, but I'm always home by the time Samantha returns from school." Next to her she perceived a small but audible sigh of impatience, and she ignored it with regal poise. She was proud of the way she balanced her life. She didn't see what could possibly be irritating about it.

"I understand you're divorced, Mrs. Carpenter," Biff noted, referring to a prep sheet on his desk. Angie nodded complacently. He looked up and regarded her shrewdly. "That means, then, that you have one less job than you used to have, doesn't it? Since you are no longer a wife, doesn't that make you an unusual candidate for a contest of this sort?"

Angie was surprised. She had been told to expect a "sweetheart" interview, meaning that Biff Marvin would not give her a hard time. She prepared to give him a polite answer, but her daughter broke in.

"That's not fair," Samantha protested self-righteously. "A Supermom means any kind of mom. It wouldn't be fair if they only allowed regular married people to be in the contest." She looked at the host with a confidential air. "You don't have to be married to be a mom, you know."

Angie blanched, and the infuriating man next to her smirked broadly. "My ex-husband and I were divorced amicably seven years ago," she said hurriedly. "I began my column not long after that. Besides," she added firmly, "I don't think that I have one less job than I used to. Marriage is a mutual relationship, not a job. And it certainly isn't a 'job' for *women* any more than it is for men."

The host looked at her with new respect. Score one for the Supermom, she thought wryly. "It's interesting," Biff remarked, deftly changing the subject, "that your career is so closely related to your life as a homemaker. Did you begin to create household hints to make housecleaning easier?"

"Not exactly. Just to make things more practical. Being a homemaker is a very creative job, and things are always hopping. You really have to be on your toes."

"Mom's a real inventor," Samantha put in enthusiastically.

Kyle Bennett laughed. "I see we have something in common." His voice was oddly intimate, pitched low but somehow very intense.

"Hardly," Angie countered, keeping her voice light and favoring him with a crushing sidelong glance. "I'm talking about taking pride in being a homemaker."

"So? I take pride in Benny."

Angie looked at the robot sitting patiently at her feet and shook her head resolutely. "I don't need a robot to do my work."

"Oh, but you do, Supermom," Kyle smiled. "You have a toaster at home, don't you?"

"Well, yes, but—"

"As well as a blender, a dishwasher, a vacuum cleaner, and a food processor, right?"

She was obliged to turn in her seat and face him, gazing directly into his disconcerting blue eyes. "So?" she asked defiantly.

"Those are all robots of a sort."

"He's got you there, Mom," Samantha said gleefully. "Irrefragably."

"Irre-what?" Angie and Biff both asked in unison.

Kyle spoke up with authoritative calm. "Irrefragably," he repeated. "It means that there's no argument to refute what I just said."

Samantha nodded solemnly, and the audience laughed.

"Okay, professor," Angie lit into him. "Let me ask you something."

He folded his arms and waited leisurely for her question, as if nothing she could say could possibly faze him.

"You claim that this machine can do anything a homemaker can do," she stated flatly.

"Within practical means."

"Can it cook a soufflé?"

"Of course." Kyle grinned. "Benny knows over a hundred recipes—everything from gourmet sauces to pizza and hamburgers." He smiled down at Samantha, who was gazing up at him in awe. "Can your mom beat that?"

"As a matter of fact, I can," Angie jumped in before Samantha could contradict her. "I know at least that many recipes, probably more. But many of mine have been personally developed by me. Can your contraption create?"

"It doesn't have to," he answered blandly.

Angie gave him a cunning little smile. "Obviously, Mr. Bennett," she said coolly, "you know nothing about the realities of running a house. I can see you've never really tried it. You think it's merely a routine bunch of mechanical chores."

"More or less," he agreed nonchalantly. "I have analyzed the components of housekeeping down to a science, and I have found that just about everything the homemaker does can be mechanized."

The women in the audience began to grumble, and the host's eyes lit up. Inflammatory statements meant higher ratings, and Angie knew he would do nothing to discourage the rivalry. Worse, she was keenly aware of the way Kyle's eyes were raking subtly but slyly over her entire body. His forthright intelligence was so compelling that she almost felt trapped—if it weren't for the way her own eyes were irresistibly drawn to the long, restless lines of his body as well. The first stirrings of an unbidden desire were winding their way into her blood, and she could have sworn that the predatory look in his clear eyes came from the same primitive source.

But his inflammatory statement had to be dealt with, and she wasn't getting any help from Biff Marvin. She twisted around in her seat to face Kyle directly, stifling her feminine reaction to him. "You couldn't be more wrong," she said with conviction. "Homemaking is a highly creative and demanding profession. It takes skill, ingenuity, patience, and planning." Samantha, sandwiched between them, was looking back and forth like a spectator at a tennis game. "Not to mention love," Angie finished in a triumphant tone. "And *that* is something your friend here couldn't provide in a million years." This brought a burst of approving applause, and she clenched her hands together to keep them from trembling.

"I'm not denying that." Kyle shrugged, quite clearly unimpressed with her argument. But something in his face had changed. He met her slightly flushed countenance with a look that would melt steel. "But you are confusing human relationships with simple, mindless chores." He looked her up and down, boldly assessing her. A hot flash of response shot through her, and she clamped her teeth together to remain calm. "Come on, now," he chided, with a slow, teasing smile. "Can't you admit that it would be nice to have a little help?"

"You're missing the point!" Angie cried, forgetting to keep calm. "I'm not saying that assistance isn't welcome. But you're not talking about 'a little help.' You're talking total replacement!"

Kyle sighed and unfolded his arms. "The fact is that

Benny here *can* do everything you can do in the house—and he can do it without these unwarranted outbursts of emotion."

Angie's eyes narrowed. That wasn't fair, and he knew it. If he was going to play rough, he was in for a big surprise. She was not going to play the sweet-tempered all-American girl next door, despite the rosy image projected by the contest. "That," she said emphatically, "is precisely my point. A home—a real home—cannot be maintained without taste, care, and warmth. In short, you can't run a house *without* emotion."

"I believe you are overrating your position," Kyle said smugly, making her want to scream. His blue eyes danced with amusement. "Again, the result of unscientific, untested opinion prompted by emotion rather than reason. I am merely saying that this Supermom juggling act of yours isn't really necessary. Much of your work can be done by a machine, and I'm sorry if that threatens you, but it happens to be true. If it can happen to men in industrial jobs, why can't it happen on the domestic scene as well?"

"Are you insinuating that the American housewife is a—" She struggled through her anger to find the proper choice of words. "—Is a—"

"—an unskilled, overrated member of a thankless and payless workforce. In short," Kyle summed up, looking straight into the camera, "the profession known as housewife is anything but a profession. It certainly isn't a career, and as far as any substantial rewards, well..." He shrugged disparagingly.

Biff Marvin tried to restore order as a loud murmur of protest arose from the audience. "Now, folks." He chuckled. "I'm sure what Mr. Bennett meant is—"

"Oh, hush!" Angie cut in, dropping the last shreds of her reserve. "We all know exactly what he meant." She faced the host accusingly. "What I don't understand is why you purposely had me on right after this character—" she jerked a thumb toward Kyle—"when you knew he was planning on making a laughingstock of my time-honored values."

"Now, wait a minute," Kyle jumped in, grabbing her arm. It was a harmless gesture, but to Angie it felt like a bolt of fire. "Don't blame it on him. He can't help it if my arguments are more persuasive."

"More—!?" Angie almost exploded with rage.

Keenly aware of the fact that he had lost control of the show, Biff Marvin hastily grabbed a box of laundry detergent from behind his desk and held it up in front of the camera. Over the squabble continuing next to him, he said loudly, "We'll be back with the battle of the homemakers after a word from our sponsor."

"CUT!" the director's voice called out from the booth perched high above the back of the audience. "Sixty seconds!"

"Whoa..." Biff let out a harried sigh. "I may be getting lost in the shuffle, but you two are doing great."

"Diaphonically," Samantha commented dryly.

Angie ignored her, but Kyle's eyes lit up in amusement. "That's some kid you've got there," he said to Angie.

"That is the first civil thing you've said to me," she retorted, refusing to fall for his bait. "Fortunately, we can't get children from robots, or are you working on that next?"

He lounged back carelessly in his seat and regarded her shrewdly. The intelligence and vitality gave him an air that was strangely powerful. "I didn't mean to insult you, Angie," he said quietly. His use of her name sent a little tingle through her, and she realized for the first time how dangerous this man could be. He could summon a deep longing in her just by looking at her in that intense way of his. She would have to be on guard.

She tried to stare back at him levelly, but it was very hard to do. His eyes were like magnets, drawing her in and keeping her under his spell. "Why didn't you say that on the air?" she challenged him. She meant to sound firm, but the words came out in a surprisingly wistful tone.

"Why don't we have a real contest?" he proposed suddenly. "You against Benny. It would be great publicity," he added persuasively.

Angie blinked in surprise. She had been right about him; she never knew when he was going to throw her a curve ball. "I'm not going to put on a show just to help promote that robot," she answered firmly.

"Then do it to promote your column," he said promptly.

"Five seconds!"

"Come on, Supermom," Kyle goaded her, fastening his unraveling gaze on her. "Are you afraid you'll lose?"

"Three, two..."

Biff turned toward the camera. "We're back!"

"What you're asking me to do," Angie said in a heated whisper, barely heeding Biff or the cameras, "is to compete in a contest with this inanimate pet of yours."

Biff's ears perked up when he heard Angie's words, and he picked up the cue as if it had been preplanned. "A contest," he repeated, making Angie blanch. "Now, that sounds interesting. Supermom versus Benny the Robot."

"Forget it," Angie said. "I'm a columnist, not a game-show contestant."

"But you're also a Supermom," Kyle insisted. "And right now your title is being challenged." He looked down at the robot. "How about it, Benny? Are you ready to take on Supermom?"

For once, the know-it-all Benny didn't answer. The lights glowed steadfastly in his mechanical brain.

"Benny!" Kyle ordered. "Shake hands!"

The mechanical arm extended up toward Angie, the challenge hanging clearly before her.

"Clamp on, Benny!" Kyle urged, forcing his point.

The mechanical claw found Angie's wrist and gripped it with programmed determination.

"Now shake!" Kyle's voice was so authoritative, so confident, that Angie jerked her hand free from the robot's grasp. Benny obediently shook the air in front of him, and Angie threw Kyle a triumphant glance.

"I don't think—" he started to say, but Angie cut him off like a knife.

"Kyle!" she barked in a deadpan imitation of his commands. "Be quiet! Now!"

The audience, which had been hanging on every word and waiting to see who would come out on top, broke into spontaneous laughter followed by a round of hearty applause, and Angie gave Kyle a chillingly sweet smile over her daughter's head.

Chapter Two

THE DAYS FOLLOWING *The Biff Marvin Show* were filled with frenzied interviews and persistent reporters who had managed to find Angie's unlisted phone number. They all wanted to know about Kyle Bennett's challenge and what, if anything, Angie was planning to do about it. The simple truth was that Angie had no intention of doing anything. She had decided flatly that her column and raising her daughter were enough of a challenge for her. She didn't need the unwelcome addition of a highly publicized contest between her and a glorified tin can—and a pair of devastating blue eyes.

In the end Angie was finally forced to take the phone off the hook to stop its unrelenting jangle. This allowed a quiet and uneventful weekend in which she tried to catch up on her sleep. Unfortunately, it just wasn't enough, and by Monday morning, she awoke with a groan of protest as the realities of daily life presented themselves with their usual regularity. There was nothing to do but plunge back into her routine.

A fast shower helped her to face the tasks of the day. She ran a brush through her thick blond hair and put on a simple blue and white caftan. With considerably less vigor than usual, she made her way into her daughter's room. There she found Samantha in her usual position, hidden under the covers and curled up in a large ball. "Up, young lady!" she commanded, trying to figure out what part of the large lump was her daughter's head. "Is that you in there?" she asked, knocking on the body.

"Aw, Mom, I'm still sleepy." This exchange was as familiar and automatic to mother and daughter as the bedtime rituals they had established years ago.

"Up!" Angie commanded, and in one deft motion she stripped the blanket from the bed. "Right now!" She marched across the room and pulled the shades up with a loud snap, sending Samantha cowering under the pillow in mock terror.

"Let's go, you're ten minutes late. Danny's mother is taking you to school today, and I want you to eat a hot breakfast. I'll make you some scrambled eggs."

"I *hate* eggs," came the muffled response.

"Since when?" Angie asked.

"Since Danny Shere put the hard-boiled egg his mom made him for lunch on the radiator in Mrs. Rose's math class. Yechhh! It smelled dis*gus*ting. I'll never eat another egg, ever again."

"Oh." Angie shrugged. "Then I guess you'll be eating cereal for the rest of your life." She scooped up Samantha's dirty clothes and marched them toward the laundry pile in the bathroom. "I don't hear you getting up, kiddo!" she called back.

"I'm almost up," Samantha said manipulatively. "My right foot is only inches from the floor."

"Both legs!" Angie insisted. "I want all of you out of that bed this instant!"

Angie stuffed the remaining clothes into a large laundry bag and paused, listening for signs of life from Samantha's room. Hearing nothing, she went back, laundry bag in tow, and peeked into the room to see her daughter's legs hovering over the floor while the rest of her remained stationed in the bed.

Samantha looked up coyly. "Almost out," she promised.

"If you need help, I'm sure the Tickle Monster will be glad to lend a hand."

"No! No, I'm getting up, honest! Aw, please, Mom!" But it was too late. Angie attacked her daughter with both hands, laughing and tickling and finally pinning her to the bed. Samantha shrieked with delight and wrestled her way into a sitting position. "Vanquished again," she announced, slapping her forehead in mock dismay.

"End of Round Ninety-two." Angie grinned. "Don't you know the Tickle Monster is unbeatable? Now, get dressed quick, sweetie. Mrs. Shere will be here soon."

"Do I have to go with Danny?" Samantha asked plaintively. "He is so juvenile."

Angie stifled a smile. "Why, honey, does he bother you?"

Samantha nodded vigorously, but she looked embarrassed. "He's always bugging me, Mom. He not only put his hard-boiled egg on the radiator, but sometimes he pulls my braids and tells me the dumbest jokes. Strictly third grade. I told him he's a jerk, and he just laughed."

Angie thought about that for a moment and smiled knowingly. "Well, Samantha," she explained gently, smoothing her daughter's hair, "I think what you've got here is a case of puppy love. It seems to me that Danny is really trying to tell you that he likes you."

"But that's impossible, Mom!" Samantha cried, totally unconvinced. "If he liked me, he wouldn't act like that!"

"That's how little boys act sometimes when they like someone."

Samantha suddenly perked up. "Is that why Mr. Bennett annoyed you?"

"No," Angie huffed. "It's different with grown-ups."

"I don't understand, Mom."

By now, Angie wasn't sure she did either. She looked at her daughter and gave it one last try. "I know it doesn't make sense, but feelings aren't always sensible. You know what I think?" Samantha listened, wide-eyed. "I think that if you treat Danny nicely, he'll stop teasing you. All he wants is for you to like him." She smiled. "Will you give it a try?"

"Okay." The response was muffled, but Angie could tell Samantha was relieved. She gave her a hug and said, "Get dressed now, Sam. It's almost eight o'clock."

Samantha hopped out of bed and Angie went down the hall toward the kitchen, thinking about breakfast. She stopped to glance at the bulletin board that hung on the inside of the swinging door to check that day's chores. Written neatly on an erasable card were the notes: DC, L, KF, CD, and PU 3D + 2L.

DC was dry cleaning, L was laundry, KF was kitchen floor, CD was column due, and PU 3D + 2L was short for pick up three dinners plus two lunches. Thank God she didn't have CP, which was car pool.

Next to the bulletin board was Samantha's dictionary

calendar. "June twelfth," she announced. "And the word for today is"—she squinted—"*invidious.*"

"Invidious," Samantha said confidently as she swung into the kitchen, dressed in jeans and a striped shirt. "It means someone who is consistently annoying."

"Can't you just say a nuisance?"

"Aw, Mom! It's not the same. Every word has its own particular meaning. I'm only trying to expand my horizons."

"Well..." Angie sighed. "I suppose it's not the same. A nuisance is a minor irritation, whereas anyone who deserves to be called invidious is a major pain in the—"

The doorbell interrupted her with a short, sharp ring. "I'll get it," Samantha said, jumping up. "It must be Danny's mother."

Angie heard the front door opening and glanced at the clock. "You're fifteen minutes early, Mrs. Shere," she called out. "Samantha hasn't eaten breakfast yet."

There was an unnaturally long pause, and then Angie discovered that it wasn't Mrs. Shere.

"Hi," came a maddeningly cheerful voice from the archway into the kitchen. "Mind if I come in?"

Standing in the entrance was Kyle Bennett. He was dressed casually in jeans and a plaid shirt, but he still looked completely confident and filled with energy.

Angie felt a sudden and unexpected bolt of electricity. Kyle's blue eyes assessed her candidly, and her half-awake state immediately vanished. She didn't know how he managed to affect her so powerfully, but instantly every nerve ending was on guard. She glanced involuntarily at Samantha's calendar. Invidious, she pronounced in her head.

"Look who's here, Mom," Samantha announced brightly, breaking the silence. "I'm having breakfast," she said to Kyle. "Want some?" Kyle's eyes twinkled, but he said nothing, instead looking at Angie for confirmation.

She had to say something. The man was standing in her kitchen uninvited, and she was only just out of bed. "Don't you believe in calling first?" she sputtered.

"I tried calling for two days, but the line was always busy. Now I see why." Kyle strolled over to where the wall phone lay dangling by its cord, then lifted it up and gently placed the receiver back on the hook. "I'll bet you were getting as many calls as I was, huh?"

"We had TV people here and everything," Samantha said excitedly. "It was really bedlam."

"I'll bet it was." Kyle nodded, but he wasn't looking at Samantha, he was looking at Angie. The electricity in his eyes was mesmerizing. "It was also great publicity. I saw your mother on the six o'clock news. She looked terrific." He smiled lazily, and Angie swallowed hard. She had never known a man who could make her melt with a mere smile—and first thing in the morning at that. "As I recall," he continued smoothly, "you were saying something about my mechanical fixation—or was it about my mechanized sensation?"

"You had it right the first time," Angie assured him, wanting to keep a firm check on the conversation before it led into realms she was not prepared to handle—especially in front of her daughter.

Kyle folded his arms and looked her up and down. She remembered that frank, unraveling gaze all too well. "Why do I get the feeling, Mrs. Carpenter, that you don't approve of me?"

"Oh, I don't know." She fluffed her hair back airily, hiding her reaction. "Maybe it's because you decided to drop in before breakfast, which is not exactly my best time." She turned to face him. "Or maybe it's because I have the distinct feeling you're going to start haranguing me about that contest idea of yours again."

He unfolded his arms and walked toward her. "It's hardly my fault if I can't reach you on the phone after you took it off the hook," he pointed out sensibly. "And you're quite right about my intentions. I have every intention of convincing you to do that contest. After all, it will be good for all of us." He winked at Samantha and, turning around, clapped his hands for attention. "So, what do you say we make the best out of this Monday morning? I haven't had my breakfast yet. How about some eggs?"

"Go right ahead." Angie smirked. "I can use a day off."

"I didn't mean that I'd cook," Kyle said.

"Just what did you mean?"

There was a momentary silence as Kyle moved away from the stove. Bowing, he gestured grandly. "It's all yours, *madame*."

"Oh, no, you don't." She stood her ground, refusing to budge. "I'm not your slave. If you want breakfast, then cook it yourself."

"But I don't cook!"

Angie let that statement sink in for a few seconds. "You don't cook?" she repeated, incredulous.

"No." He looked quite complacent, as if his attitude were perfectly normal.

Samantha giggled.

"Without meaning to be personal," Angie began again,

"just how do you manage to eat, if you don't cook?"

Kyle shrugged. "I eat out," he said, as if any idiot should have known. "Although lately Benny has been making me a few things."

"Benny is your cook?"

"Sometimes."

"And the other times," Angie said faintly, "you just ... eat out?"

"Why not?" he shrugged. "Besides, Benny hates doing dishes."

"Me, too," Samantha chimed in.

Angie didn't say anything. She was trying to figure out what kind of lifestyle Kyle Bennett actually led. Obviously, a real bachelor's life. "I assume you have laundry?" she couldn't resist asking. "Plus a home to keep clean, a bed to make..." Somehow she couldn't picture him doing anything as mundane as making a bed. But did that robot really do everything? She just couldn't believe it.

As if sensing her thoughts, Kyle said, "If you're trying to ascertain just how much time I spend at household chores, the answer is zero." He made a zero with his fingers for emphasis.

"Then who—"

Kyle put his hand up to stop her from continuing. "Dirty clothes," he explained, "are dropped off at the local laundry in the morning and picked up in the afternoon, washed and folded. My apartment is cleaned by Benny, and as far as what's left, well—" He shrugged carelessly. "I manage."

"Ummm," was all Angie could muster. She got up and poured Samantha a bowl of cereal, put a piece of bread in the toaster, and began making eggs.

Behind her, she could sense Kyle's exploration of her

kitchen. She could hear him picking up certain household items and gadgets, examining them with scientific curiosity. "What's this?" he asked, picking up a salad spinner that was sitting on the counter.

"You wash lettuce and then spin it around to dry it," Angie informed him vaguely.

"Oh, I see," he nodded. "Centrifugal force, and the water is trapped on the outside. Clever." He didn't sound all that interested, and she had the uneasy feeling that she was being patronized.

"If you read my column, which somehow I seriously doubt, you might learn something about the science of homemaking." She knew she sounded defensive, but she couldn't help it. Just because he was some kind of genius inventor didn't give him the right to make fun of her.

"Science?" he questioned, confirming her suspicion. "Are you comparing the housewife to a scientist?"

"Homemaker," Angie insisted. "And yes, I am. Do you have any idea how much science is a part of keeping a house in order?"

"Of course, but to a degree."

"No *buts* about it," Angie continued. "Take laundry."

"Okay," he shrugged. "What about it?"

"Have you ever tried to get a very tough stain out of a fabric?"

"You forget, I don't do my own laundry."

"But when you did," she pressed.

He gave her a disarming grin. "I never did laundry—ever! I wouldn't even know how."

On that note, Angie turned back to her eggs, which were now overcooked. "You don't have to sound so proud of it," she mumbled to herself.

"Did you say something?"

Angie didn't answer. She dished out the eggs and went to pour some juice. There was a long pause.

"Uh—where's mine?" Kyle asked, evidently already suspecting the answer.

Angie pointed wordlessly to the refrigerator.

"All right," he said with an injured air. "I'll make a go of it."

He went up to the refrigerator, and after selecting two eggs from the carton, he bravely proceeded to prepare them. The eggs went into a bowl along with a few stray bits of shell. He beat them vigorously with a fork and dumped them into the pan, forgetting to add butter first. Samantha watched wide-eyed and Angie pretended not to watch at all. When at last his eggs were ready, he had a hard time scraping them out of the pan and onto a plate.

"Kyle, your eggs got stuck," Samantha observed candidly.

Angie took a good look at the pan and tried hard to repress a giggle. "You really *don't* know how to cook, do you?" she asked coolly.

"I don't see what you're so upset about," he said as he set the plate on the table with a flourish. "These are eggs à la Bennett."

"As long as they aren't eggs à la Benny," Angie mumbled. She was positive that any moment he was going to start manipulating her again, and she had decided it might be wise to take the offensive.

Kyle caught the remark and looked up sharply. "Now, that was uncalled for," he said primly. "I don't see why you should have anything against Benny. He's perfectly harmless."

"I don't have anything against him," she said truthfully. "I have something against *you*." This remark came out sounding much ruder than she had intended, and she looked down to hide her surprise at her own bluntness.

"I see." He sat down to join them, seemingly unperturbed by her ungracious remark. "But since I am, after all, Benny's creator, Benny and I are in many ways one and the same. And do you know what else I think, Supermom?" He leaned forward and gave her a chilly smile. "I think you feel threatened by Benny. You put homemaking on a pedestal because you're afraid, deep down, that you really can't do anything else."

"That is not true!" she cried, jumping up and almost upsetting the untouched plate of eggs. "I also have a career. You know that. How dare you come into my home first thing in the morning and start criticizing me?"

The menacing glare went out of him like a flame extinguished in a strong wind. He shrugged. "It was worth a shot. I told you I would get you to participate in that contest by hook or crook."

She sat down heavily. "You mean you were just saying all that to get my goat?" He nodded complacently, and she swallowed hard. He didn't seem to realize that he had touched a tender spot in her. All her life, Angie had striven to be exemplary—first as a cheerful, cooperative girl, then as a devoted wife, and finally as a caring, loving mother. She had never completely lived down the fact that she had been Miss Apple Blossom in high school, because the title had fit her so perfectly. Miss Apple Blossom Supermom, she thought ruefully, studying Kyle carefully. But apparently he wasn't aware of the ammunition he had discovered, and she wasn't about to tell him. "You are a very strange man, you know that?" she said, feigning disapproval.

His cheerful grin returned. "I know. I'm not very good

at convincing people. I go right for the jugular. You'll have to forgive me; it's the only way I know to get what I want." The considerable charm and flair with which he delivered this speech were so sudden and so startling that Angie just stared at him, her mouth half open.

Samantha was watching both of them with keen awareness. Something was going on here that transcended a mere argument, and evidently she felt that her encouragement would be helpful. "Why do you want my mom to be in that contest so much, Mr. Bennett?" she asked winsomely.

"Call me Kyle," he said with an engaging smile. "And the answer is simple. I need the publicity. Benny is a six-handed marvel, and I have no doubt of his potential popularity. But he's also expensive, and he took me six long years to develop and create." His tone became even more persuasive, and his blue eyes took on an intensity that was unsettling. Angie squirmed as she felt his power at work. "Right now I can use all the help I can get. The attention we've both been receiving since that television show is only the beginning if we play our cards right."

Angie took a deep breath and gave him a penetrating look. He was too fast, too smooth, too sure of himself to be real. "You know what I think?" she asked shrewdly. "I think you're a kook. A loner. An oddball who is so stuck on a piece of fancy machinery that he can't see anything else in front of his nose." This time her bluntness was quite deliberate, and she had no intention of backing down.

Two things happened simultaneously at this crucial juncture. The doorbell rang, and black smoke began pouring abruptly out of the toaster.

"It's Mrs. Shere," Samantha announced. "Bye-bye,

everybody." She jumped up and headed out through the swinging doors yelling, "Coming!" at the top of her lungs.

"Don't forget your lunch box," Angie called after her. She hurried over to the toaster, fanning the smoke with her hands.

"Now look what you made me do."

Kyle came up behind her and jerked the plug from the wall.

"No one can make you do anything," he said lightly. "Especially not me. I seem to be learning that the hard way."

Angie was profoundly embarrassed. She could only imagine what he was thinking, especially after her grand speech. A Supermom wasn't supposed to do things like burn toast. Kyle gingerly held the blackened mess over the sink.

"Nothing left here but carbon compound," he said, tossing the remains delicately into the garbage.

"I forgot all about that stupid toaster," Angie muttered. "It has to be watched." She looked at Kyle and shrugged. "I guess I should have it fixed, right?"

He was examining the toaster gravely. "Ah, here's the problem," he said after a moment. He put a knife into the side of the toaster and began twisting it. "The Thermoconductors are worn. I'll have to replace them later."

"What? No, you won't," Angie sputtered, following him back to the table. "Do you think you can walk in here and take over my life, just like that?"

Kyle shrugged casually. "I don't know. Probably not. But it would be nice," he added, almost as an afterthought. He wheeled around to face her, the casualness gone. His hands moved to her arms, holding her gently but firmly. "Let's face it, Angie. That contest is important, and I'm going to keep persuading you until you agree to do it. I have a feeling we may get more out of it than we bargained for." He stopped talking, but his hands remained where they were, firmly holding her in front of him. Now that she was this close to him, Angie's heart began beating at an alarming rate. She wondered nervously if he was aware of her galloping pulse. She knew that she was keenly aware of his uncompromising stance, the way his legs were thrust forward, and the air of predetermined victory that seemed to hover over his well-placed head like an invisible halo. His head bent to gaze directly into her eyes, and his hands tightened intimately on her arms. "Admit it," he said huskily. "You want to do it."

"Do what?" she whispered breathlessly, and in that one unfortunate double entendre, she knew she was lost. A sly twinkle stole into his eyes, and the inches between them disappeared.

"You'd better stop me now, Angie," he murmured, his lips against hers, "or you won't be able to stop me at all."

Chapter Three

ANGIE WAS LOST in a swirl of sensation as he kissed her, slowly and sweetly and with a great sense of inevitability. The storm that had been building between them ever since they had met was at last breaking. At first she was too stunned to do anything but stand trapped in his embrace, but then the sweetly sinuous flames began to rise up and claim her. It had been so long, so very, very long, she thought in a rush of abandon as her arms entwined around his neck. It wasn't that no one had kissed her in seven years; she had dated from time to time since her divorce. But no other man had summoned even a fraction of the response that Kyle was commanding in her at this moment. She scarcely knew what she was doing, and for once she didn't care. For seven long years, she had been the cheerful, competent, reliable Supermom, juggling the house, her daughter, her column. Now, for once in her well-ordered life, she would allow herself to submit to an unbridled passion that was lurking beneath her cool surface.

Kyle perceived her surrender at once. His strong arms held her easily as his mouth, warm and insistent, began a tantalizing journey over her cheeks, her nose, her eyelids, and her ear. Only when he was sure that she was powerless to resist did he claim her mouth again, taking her tongue this time as well. Honey and fire flowed between them, and time became suspended as they clung to each other.

"Mmmm," he murmured after a long, delicious moment. "I knew it would be this good."

Angie blinked as she managed to catch her breath. Was this the real reason he had come? "You mean you've been... thinking about doing this?" she asked.

"Of course," he answered huskily. "I told you I was going to win, Angie. And if you think I was just talking about the contest, then you've been hiding from the obvious."

Angie didn't know what to say. Now that she had kissed him, now that they had both crossed the indelible line that separated restraint from open sensuality, she didn't know if she would ever be able to think of him in any other way.

"I—I didn't think..." she began, but her voice trailed off in bewilderment. Then she took a good look at him and got a firmer grip on herself. The self-assured glint that was replacing the tenderness in his eyes sparked her back to reality. She couldn't allow herself to be swept away so easily. If he thought she was going to be an easy conquest, he had better think again. "I didn't think this was a necessary part of the bargain," she said in a clear tone.

Anything Goes 35

He laughed gently. "Necessary? Probably not." His eyes glowed with masculine desire. "But definitely inevitable."

Before she could think of a suitable comeback, he kissed her again, and this time there was a definite air of triumph in his movements.

"Are you sure?" Angie retorted the moment the kiss had ended.

"Yes," he said firmly, cupping her face between his hands. "Trust me, Angie." He bent to kiss her one more time, but she wriggled out of his grasp.

"How can I trust you when you have sworn to finagle me into doing that ridiculous contest?" she demanded.

"But that's just the point," he said earnestly. "I've been perfectly honest about my intentions. And about my motives."

She surveyed him from head to toe, wishing desperately that he would stop looking so magnetically appealing for one fraction of a second so that she could think clearly.

"But what about your motives with *me*?" she said at last.

He threw his hands up in a gesture of innocence. "My intentions are honorable, madam," he declared in a parody of an old-fashioned suitor. Then his blue eyes hardened into a predatory glint. "I am going to make love to you, Angie Carpenter, and you are going to be a very willing partner. That I guarantee."

"This is too much!" she exclaimed, backing away from him in disbelief, even though she felt an involuntary tremor of excitement deep inside herself at his words. "You sound like something out of an old movie."

A slight shadow crossed his face, but it disappeared just as quickly. "I know," he admitted readily. "I told you I'm not very good at convincing people." The sensual glint returned. "But I am good at making things happen."

They stared at each other for a moment in silence, her stubbornness matching his determination. Here she was, alone in her home with a man who could arouse her with one careless touch, and it all seemed so easy. It was the perfect fantasy—a tryst with the handsome stranger. Except that Kyle wasn't really a stranger, and fantasies don't have the consequences that real-life scenarios do. The moment passed, and Kyle broke the spell.

"Okay," he said quietly. "I'll back off—for now. But you need me, Angie, and when you realize that, I'll be here."

"That's very gallant of you," she said breathlessly. "But not all that perceptive. I've been managing quite well on my own for several years now."

"Managing is not what I had in mind."

Again there was a subtle pause, but nothing more was said, and after a long moment, Angie turned nervously to clear the breakfast dishes. She was keenly aware of Kyle's presence. He was standing only a few feet in back of her, and she was positive that he was watching her every move. "Would you like some coffee?" she suggested abruptly.

"Why not?"

Glad for something to do, Angie quickly put the coffee on as Kyle sat down again. A few moments of neutral silence passed between them, and she felt heartened enough to ask him something that had been bothering her. "Kyle? Do you mind if I ask you . . . I mean, I don't want to sound rude, but—well, what exactly do you do for a living?" It sounded awkward to her, but Kyle looked mildly surprised.

"No, I don't mind your asking," he said. "Why should I?"

"It's just that you don't seem to be very...conventional," she explained. "I wondered if—well, if you actually did anything at all."

"Well, of course I do," he answered, sounding vaguely annoyed. "I'm an inventor."

Angie stared at him. "You mean like Thomas Edison?"

"Something like that. But adapted to the computer age."

Angie didn't know what to say. She had never met an inventor before. To her, inventors were in the same league as Benjamin Franklin. "What—what have you invented?" she asked finally, hoping to sound reasonably intelligent about it.

Kyle answered readily. "Our biggest achievement was doubling the memory capacity in microchips. But right now we're working on laser-driven robots for space exploration."

"Gosh." Angie wanted to bite her tongue the moment she said it. Now he would think she was a real lamebrain. But it wasn't an everyday occurrence to meet someone who talked casually about robots in space. She barely knew what to say as she poured the coffee quickly and sat down.

But Kyle didn't seem to notice her sudden reticence. He was thinking hard about something, and he sipped his coffee intently as she studied him. "If those guys at NASA don't meet our price, we'll be shopping around. Benny is our real star, but we need that damn contract from NASA to get him going." He seemed to be talking to himself, his fingers unconsciously drumming the table.

"And that's why you want to do this contest," Angie interjected tactfully.

"What?" He looked up sharply. "Oh, right. And then we've got to run down to Washington..." Again he was abruptly lost in thought, and Angie had a sudden sinking glimmer of recollection. She knew what it was like to live with a man who never stopped thinking about his work. She knew because she was divorced from one, and the last thing she wanted was to relive that monotonously gray period of her life. Her cup clattered to its saucer and she mentally willed Kyle to look at her.

Mercifully, he did. He drained his cup and gave her a tiny smile, almost as if he had been caught by surprise. "You know, you look beautiful at this hour of the morning," he said softly, as if noticing her for the first time, and Angie almost fell off her chair. Kyle was so unpredictable that she barely knew what to make of him. "Don't look so surprised," he added calmly.

"Well, but I—I can't help it," she stammered. "You—you're not thinking about me one second, and then the next you fix me with that passionate gaze." She thought her words would wipe the hungry expression off his face, but he continued to rake her body with his disconcerting eyes.

"You're quite distracting," he explained calmly, but she detected an undercurrent of sensuality that unnerved her.

"I'm not trying to be," she said honestly.

"I know." His voice dropped a level, becoming huskier as he studied her face. Any other man would have embarrassed her, looking at her so candidly this early in the day. She wasn't wearing any makeup, her hair was disheveled, and her loose caftan was comfortable but not particularly flattering. Nevertheless, Kyle was looking at her as if she were the most desirable woman on earth, and it was difficult not to bask in the rays he transmitted. "I know you're not trying to be," he repeated, "and that's exactly what's so sexy about it. You're seducing me, Angie, and you don't even know it. You could drive a man mad."

His words sparked something deep within her, and her body responded against her will. It was if he were making love to her without touching her, using only his words and the penetrating blue of his eyes. Angie fought back the color she knew was rising to her cheeks and willed herself to breathe normally, but suddenly her legs felt like rubber and her breasts seemed to rise of their own accord and swell against the thin fabric of her caftan. Their delicate peaks hardened into sensitive points, and she wondered feverishly if Kyle could tell.

But his eyes were fastened on her slightly parted lips, tracing the lush lines with obvious male hunger. "We both know what would happen if I kissed you now," he said. "I wouldn't be able to stop, would I?"

Transfixed, Angie breathlessly shook her head.

"And then I'd be kissing your neck and your throat and holding you close enough to explore every inch of your beautiful body." She caught her breath and swallowed hard.

Kyle took in her reaction with a tight little smile. "You're not ready for this yet. I can see that. You want me, but you don't understand why." A glimmer of regret crossed his magnetic, irregular features, but it quickly changed to anticipation. "When you do, I'll be more than ready to oblige you."

"What do you want from me?" Angie demanded in a

hoarse whisper. "Why do you come into my home and talk to me this way? You have no right!"

"I know I don't," he broke in gently, his eyes never leaving her face. "But I am merely stating the truth. I told you, Angie, I'm a blunt man. Don't expect me to court you with posies and standoffish games. When I see something I want, I go after it. I've never played anything according to the rules, and I don't intend to start now."

Somehow, in the midst of her swirling desire, she was able to conjure up a protest. "You may have to," she informed him as levelly as she could. "I'm not a toy for the taking. You won't be able to manipulate me into your life or your bed. I'm a grown woman with a child. I can't allow myself to be carried away by impetuous whims."

"This isn't impetuous, and it isn't a whim," he answered. "You can't deny the current that is flashing between us at this very moment. It's been there from the beginning."

"But you're talking about physical attraction," she blurted out. "That's hardly the basis for a relationship."

A twinkle stole into his eyes, but his mouth didn't smile. "I never said anything about a relationship," he announced, "although I'm sure there are relationships based on far less."

Angie was incensed. "Then what *do* you want?" she cried. "A quick roll in the hay with a lonely divorcée? Is *that* what this is all about?"

For once, Kyle's composure was broken. He actually looked shocked, she noted with a surge of satisfaction. "Don't say that, Angie," he admonished. "I didn't mean—"

"I think it's about time you made yourself clear," she said icily.

A flash of anger darted across his face for a moment, but he quickly dismissed it and leaned forward earnestly. "I don't want to play games, Angie. I want you, and I know you want me. What will happen in the future, I can't say. I'm not a prophet."

"You seem to think you are! You've got a whole sizzling scenario already mapped out." Her eyes were blazing, and she shifted slightly in her seat in an attempt to quell the desire that was still coursing through her.

He leaned back and regarded her shrewdly. "Don't fool yourself, Angie. You've been running hot and cold on me since we met, and I'm not buying it. Maybe you're shy, or maybe it's been a long time for you. I don't care. We are going to resolve this thing, and I'm willing to wait until you're ready to face it like the woman I know you are."

"That's very gracious of you," she said dryly, but he didn't take the bait.

"Thank you," he said magnanimously, inclining his head. "I knew you'd see it my way."

"You are an impossible man," she muttered.

"Oh, I know. I like being impossible. Although I prefer to see it as simply having high standards."

Angie almost choked, and she debated ordering him flatly out of her house. She didn't know how much longer she could maintain her composure and she desperately wanted to avoid making a fool of herself. As drawn as she was to him, she felt the need to keep him at bay. He was a free spirit, footloose and independent. Surely he had no real place in her well-ordered life.

At that moment, the doorbell rang, shattering the spell that had entwined them. Angie started nervously, and Kyle sat back impatiently, throwing her a quizzical glance. She shook her head innocently; she wasn't expecting anyone. But the identity of the caller was quickly revealed. A series of determined knocks was followed by a shrill voice that rang right through the door. "Yoohooo! Anybody home? Angie, dear, it's me, Britt." More pounding followed as Britt doggedly continued. "Angie? Are you there?"

"Who's that?" Kyle asked, as if the visitor had come from another planet. The doorbell was jabbed again, making them both jump. *"What* is that?"

"That," Angie explained resignedly as she headed to the door, "is the self-appointed guardian of Supermom."

The door swung open to reveal the editor of *Modern Woman* magazine, Britt Shapiro Whittaker. She was a tiny whirlwind of a woman who had the look of someone who has been painstakingly manufactured. Her mane of hair was artfully colored to a gingery shade, her makeup was flawlessly designed to camouflage the hint of middle age, and her pert nose had been skillfully shaped by a fashionable Park Avenue plastic surgeon. She was wearing a peach-colored silk dress and a tasteful string of pearls, but her manicured fingers sported several large rings with glittering stones.

"I *tried* calling, love," she cooed, knowing that she was intruding but still intent on entering, "but there's something wrong with your phone, and—" She stopped short when she caught sight of Kyle. "Well, now, isn't *this* a coincidence! You're the very reason for my visit." She turned back to Angie, her eyes narrowing. "I hope you haven't agreed to anything until I look at the contract."

Kyle was staring strangely at Britt, but Angie threw up her hands in defeat. "Why do I have the feeling there's a conspiracy going on here?" she demanded.

"Don't look at me," he said innocently. "I just came over for a free breakfast, remember?"

"I suggest we all sit down and discuss the details," Britt said, and marched into the living room to make herself comfortable.

Kyle filed in after her, leaving Angie standing alone. "I've got a column due by the end of today," she protested.

"Which is one of the reasons I'm here," Britt said. "You're going to have to spruce up those household hints a little."

"What do you mean, spruce up?" Angie asked irritably.

"They're too *common*," Britt explained. "Now that you've become a television celebrity, you've got to come up with something a little *jazzier*."

"Oh, I don't know," Kyle said with a straight face, "I think Angie is pretty jazzy already. How jazzy can a person get?"

Angie tried to give him the evil eye and nod at the same time, succeeding only in looking utterly perplexed.

"We're also changing the name of your column," Britt added.

"We?" Angie looked at Kyle quizzically, but he merely looked blank.

"Yes, I already cleared it with your paper. From now on you'll be nationally syndicated as 'Supermom'."

"I like that," Kyle noted. "It's jazzy, all right."

"Have you two dreamboats worked anything out between you?" Britt asked pointedly.

"Between us?" Angie repeated.

"Yes, you know—the contest between you and that cute little robot."

"There's not going to be a contest," Angie stated flatly. "And as far as changing the name of my column, that's entirely up to me."

"Of *course*," Britt said at once in saccharine tones that were coating a wall of iron. "And I have every *confidence* that your good sense will prevail, dear. As for the contest—well, you know *Modern Woman* is *sponsoring* it, and we have high hopes—"

Angie held a tight rein on her temper and mentally counted to ten. "The contest is entirely up to me," she announced firmly, "and I'm saying no. And that's final."

The phone rang, breaking into her ultimatum, and Kyle was instantly on guard. "Ten A.M. on the dot," he announced, consulting his watch. "That's my partner calling." He marched into the kitchen to answer it, his body tense with anticipation, leaving a startled Angie to face Britt alone.

"Now, about the contest?" Britt continued as if Angie hadn't spoken at all. "I think I can get a friend of mine to lend us two brand-new houses on Long Island. Of course, we'll need time for promotion and that sort of thing, but..."

While Britt rambled on and on about the rules of the contest and some kind of prize, Angie held her tongue and watched as Kyle took his call.

"Yeah?" he answered tersely. This was followed by several curt nods, punctuated by more *yeahs*. "They want *what*?" he demanded at one point. He ran his hand through his hair in frustration. "Then you'll be there. Get those papers in order and meet me at the terminal." He slammed down the phone without saying good-bye and was suddenly filled with the same restless energy Angie had first noticed in him. "Damn that—" Kyle stopped himself from cursing when he saw the two women gazing at him in alarm. "My partner has to fly down to Washington in an hour. I've got to go over some papers with him immediately."

Without another word, he strode to the door, his forehead creased in concentration. "I'll be in touch," he said shortly, and before Angie could say anything, he was out the door. The door closed behind him, leaving a sudden harsh silence, and Angie turned helplessly to the shrewd Britt, who had taken in the entire scene with sharp interest.

"Reminds me of my first husband," Britt mused.

She went on to talk about how lucky they both were to be divorced, because now they had so much more freedom. Somewhere between the history of Britt's fabulous success and the demise of her second marriage, Angie tuned out.

She was still dwelling on Kyle and what he had said about housewives and homemaking. Somehow she knew he wasn't totally wrong; it was just that his attitude definitely needed altering. It's all a matter of reeducation, she realized slowly. A new approach was needed to address the problems of household chores. Obviously, the old ways were not working, and to make matters worse, the homemaker was losing the pedestal she had maintained for decades. The job was on its way to becoming utterly thankless, and Angie was not going to let that happen.

Then it hit her.

A new idea was starting to form inside her head, and the more Britt rattled on, the better the idea got. It was born out of a mixture of anger and aggravation, sparked partly by Britt and partly by Kyle. But the motivation didn't matter. She was hot and she knew it. Britt wanted a newer, snappier column—and she was going to get it. The idea mushroomed, and in seconds she had ideas for a whole series of columns.

Suddenly, she jumped straight up. "It's brilliant!"

Britt stopped talking long enough to stare at her curiously.

"You're brilliant!" Angie cried ecstatically, forgetting her former antagonism. "Even that nut Bennett is brilliant."

A second later, she was running for her typewriter, the opening lines for her next column streaming out of her head faster than she could type them.

"Kyle Bennett," she called out happily, "prepare to meet thy match!"

Chapter Four

THE FIRST SUPERMOM column Angie wrote after her revelation had all the pizzazz of a torpedo speeding toward a target. It was titled "How to Train Your Husband," and was, she believed, guaranteed to sink a lot of ships. In it, she offered a step-by-step method to get husbands out from behind their newspapers and over to the kitchen sink. The nagging reminder of the tantalizing but ultimately hopeless Kyle Bennett was transformed into a working reality that enabled her to vent her frustrations, channel her energies, and inspire her readers, all at the same time.

Angie wondered if Kyle read that first column, and if he would know that she had written it expressly with him in mind. There were no more little impromptu visits, and he didn't try to call her, but his invisible presence remained her inspiration, and the columns continued to flow forth like water from a dam.

"How to Train Your Husband" was immediately followed by "Men and Laundry," a concise, sharp-edged piece in which she pointed out that men claim they are better than women when it comes to mechanical objects, but are somehow flustered by the many dials and switches on a washing machine. "They can always figure out how to adjust the color dial on the TV for Sunday afternoon football games," she wrote, "but they can't separate colorfast clothes. They can always dial the right channel, but when it comes to dialing permanent press on the dryer, they're suddenly all thumbs."

"Going on Strike," "Vacations for One," and "Kids: The Untapped Labor Force in Your Home" made her the number-one spokeswoman for the harried housewife. It was a distinct departure from her usual more routine hints, but her paper decided to take a chance on it, and soon, women all over the country were echoing her cries for freedom. Britt booked her onto as many TV and radio shows as she could handle, and her fame and popularity mushroomed all over again.

Not all of the responses were positive, of course. A lot of husbands began to feel the effects of their wives' new attitudes toward what Angie called "Divide and Conquer." This meant a system of dividing the chores equally in order to conquer them better and faster, but most men didn't interpret it that way. If anything, they felt threatened and conquered. This resulted in hecklers in the audiences Angie was invited to address, as well as a few minor protests. One syndicated cartoonist drew a wickedly comical caricature of her face at the center of a dart board on the wall of a tavern. Various macho types were portrayed drinking beer at the bar, and Angie's face was covered with darts that had been thrown at the board.

Despite these few incidents, Angie enjoyed her new recognition. But the pace was grueling, and at the end of a month of touring, she had had it. She wasn't used to so much traveling, she couldn't keep asking her mother to take Samantha, and even her unflappable daughter had become weary of Angie's new status.

To Britt's visible chagrin, Angie announced that she would do no more publicity for a while, except for a final hints demonstration near her home on Long Island at the Roosevelt Field shopping center.

Britt put all her formidable energies into making this final appearance a memorable one. The shopping center had a huge rotunda in front of JC Penney's, and Britt chose this area to build a small stage with a mock kitchen, a living room, and carpeted floors. A large banner with the single word SUPERMOM emblazoned across it was hung over the set, as if nothing more needed to be said to draw a huge crowd of enthusiastic fans.

Britt was right, Angie saw. The rotunda was packed an hour before the demonstration was scheduled to begin, as anxious women assured themselves a place. Britt had carefully advertised and promoted the event, but even she seemed surprised at the turnout. There had been a few sticky incidents with male hecklers and wiseacres at the last few appearances, and Britt wasn't taking any chances.

"That's why I've scheduled this one for the middle of the afternoon," she explained to Angie in confidential tones. "Men are usually *working* at that time, you know." Her sharp eyes scanned the crowd with satisfaction. "This is definitely for girls only."

She mounted the stage with coy excitement, her pink ruffly dress fluttering about her dainty knees. She took a deep breath as she surveyed the eager crowd, her tiny waist expanding for just a second, and began, "It is my honor to introduce the spokeswoman for the American housewife—" But she never got to finish her introduction, because the place went wild with cheers and applause. Angie hopped up to the stage on cue, and it was as if the volume in the rotunda had suddenly been turned up.

The crowd went crazy. Several women raised dishtowels like flags—a new symbol that had sprung up during the recent tour. Banners were unfurled, proclaiming the end of drudgery. Slogans of all kinds dotted the air like constellations: HE CAN'T WATCH THE SUPERBOWL UNTIL HE CLEANS THE TOILET BOWL. DISHPAN HANDS FOR MEN. DON'T TREAD ON ME.

"Angie! Angie! Angie!" the women chanted in unison. Cameras flashed and clicked continually, and Angie smiled back warmly at her fans, reveling in their ardent show of support.

For three very long and noisy minutes, the women continued to shout and applaud. A man would have to be out of his mind to show up at a place like this, Angie thought to herself, seeing Samantha stationed off to the side and giving her a wink. He'd stick out like a sore thumb.

She grinned at the idea and then turned her smile back to her audience. Her eyes swept over the legion of admirers like a TV camera, proudly taking everything in— when suddenly the proverbial sore thumb stuck out in the crowd. Instantly, her eyes flashed back to the lone man standing with arms folded, looking directly at her.

Oh, God, Angie thought, her heart accelerating madly as she kept the Miss America smile frozen on her face. It couldn't be.

Anything Goes

She turned away from him determinedly. Let him stay, she thought. Let him see me on my own turf, surrounded by people who appreciate what I'm saying. Her smile became even more radiant as she addressed the crowd.

"I hope you all got everything in your houses in order before coming here."

Laughter circled the open square. "My husband did it all last night!" someone yelled out.

Angie couldn't help sneaking a look at Kyle as the audience responded with hoots of laughter. He was still standing placidly with his arms folded, but she sensed the same restless energy in him that had disturbed her before. Had he come here to challenge her? If he had, she had no intention of letting him take the upper hand. These were her people, and this was her show. She was in her element here, and no one was going to take that away from her. The determination sparkled furiously in her eyes for a moment, and his face broke into a slow, teasing smile. Show me, he seemed to be saying to her.

Once again she averted her gaze, looking back to her admirers for support. He had guts coming here, she admitted to herself. These people could slaughter him.

"How's your leisure life treating you?" she called out to her fans. Again there was a series of smart answers, and this time Angie held her hand up to control the reaction.

"I've got some great new hints for you today, and I want you all to remember to share them with your husbands!" This was met with a new round of cheers, which Angie fed by standing back and nodding encouragingly.

"And let's not forget that unsung hero, the Superdad," she called out over the din. "After all, not all men are helpless clods, right?"

A new round of cheers erupted, and Angie smiled

serenely at Kyle. She waited leisurely for two whole minutes until the noise had died down, and only then did she head over to the counter to begin her demonstration.

Kyle still hadn't moved, but Angie loftily ignored him. What exactly was he doing here? Her heart jumped as she wondered if he had read her latest columns. Suddenly, she realized that the place had become totally quiet. Everyone was waiting for her to begin. She smiled quickly and marched over to the counter.

"Hint number one," she announced hurriedly, "concerns the vacuum cleaner. Remember all those times the vacuum cleaner bag was full, but you'd forgotten to buy more?" she asked the crowd. Several people nodded. "It's no problem. Watch." She produced a filled bag, picked up a pair of scissors, and cut an inch off the top. After emptying the dirt, she folded the cut ends down, then held up the bag and a stapler. "Now you can use it again," she concluded, stapling the loose ends shut.

She risked a sidelong glance at Kyle to see if he was impressed with her ingenuity and her popularity. To her consternation, she saw him waving to her daughter, who returned the greeting eagerly. Then, as if to goad her more, he ambled closer to the stage, only ten feet away.

I hope he doesn't have that six-armed tin can stashed somewhere with him, Angie thought. Before she could look away, he smiled at her suddenly, a dazzling smile that sent a bolt of blue lightning through his eyes. Angie tried valiantly to pretend she hadn't noticed, but that was impossible. He no longer looked like an interested member of the audience. She knew he had come here for a reason, and she also knew that it was only a matter of time before he revealed what it was.

Unfortunately, Kyle Bennett had given her what Samantha called the double whammy. His very presence was affecting Angie's performance. What was worse, the taunting memory of being held in his arms flew unbidden at her from the far reaches of her mind. She ordered the memory back in its corner, but every time she caught a glimpse of Kyle's enigmatic face, she couldn't help remembering how powerful and how intimate his kisses had been. And the brazen way he had spoken to her echoed in her mind no matter how staunchly she tried to forget it. Fifteen minutes into her lecture, Angie had become all thumbs. By the time she finished recycling three-way light bulbs and using a toothbrush to clean a grater, she had managed to drop a light bulb, misplace a knife, and lose an earring to the electric blender.

What really miffed her was that each time she glanced down into the audience, Kyle was a few feet closer to the stage. By the time she wound up the first half of her demonstration, she was barely in control of her act. She took a deep breath and determined to stick it out. She couldn't let a pair of blue eyes do this to her.

"Here's another common problem," she announced with renewed determination as she attacked a blended cake mix with a twin rotary mixer. "How to clean the blades?" She took out the batter-coated blades and held them up.

"Just take an ordinary shopping bag, stick the blades inside, plug them back into the mixer, and put it on high speed."

"Well, that's simple enough!"

It was Kyle's voice. As the batter splattered safely inside the bag, she looked down to see him standing at the foot of the stage. He smiled devilishly at her, and for a split second she stood mesmerized, completely forgetting her performance.

"And fascinating," he added dryly, candidly observing her discomfort.

Angie was furious. How dare he come here and sabotage her! She turned angrily back to her task, yanking out the blades a split second before the mixer had come to a stop. Instantly, she was splattered with a residue of cake batter, and the audience broke into laughter.

"Oh, my goodness!" she exclaimed. Kyle watched calmly as she grabbed a sponge and dabbed at the splotches. Remembering her audience, she looked up with a wry grin, and added, "Just remember to wait until the mixer is turned off, folks."

"Talk about egg on your face!" she overheard Kyle say.

That did it. "It's better than a foot in your mouth," Angie muttered directly to him.

Quickly, she saw that she had made a mistake. The audience caught her inhospitable remark and instantly picked up on the byplay.

What made it even worse was Kyle's apology.

"I'm sorry," he said expansively. "I guess I keep messing up your act, don't I? Now, if Benny were here, he would be glad to lend a hand."

This revelation enabled everyone to figure out exactly who he was. In no time at all, fingers were pointing to the lone man at the foot of the stage. There were giggles and whispered comments, and Angie heard one woman remark, "Oh, it's that robot fellow from the Marvin show. I wonder if they brought him here on purpose."

Angie fought back the urge to deny any such arrangement, and doggedly pursued her planned program. "Remember," she said, "homemaking is a never-ending job. You have to take time out, and I don't just mean a coffee break. It's important to schedule time for yourself and to use it productively." She proceeded to talk about the various ways in which to accomplish this, but a movement down below her distracted her, and once more she glanced involuntarily at Kyle. To her consternation, he was waving off to the side of the stage and mouthing something to Samantha. The child laughed at some joke he had managed to convey to her, but stopped cold when she saw her mother's stern face. Kyle also stopped and obediently turned his attention back to Angie.

"Now we come to the best part of our gathering," Angie announced almost ironically. "Those who have seen me on TV know that I like to have a volunteer come up and help me answer questions from the audience. So if some brave soul will—"

Kyle jumped up on the stage in one hop. "I volunteer!"

Angie almost hooted. "Not you!" she exclaimed. "Anyone but you!"

"Why not? I'm a homemaker!"

"You? A homemaker?"

Kyle put up his hands in self-defense and addressed Angie and the audience at the same time. "Any objections?"

The audience applauded his bravery as well as his obvious challenge. They knew he was there looking for a fight, and they all knew they would enjoy it.

"I don't know," Angie said darkly. "I may object to your motives." Her heart jumped as he smiled at her, and her eyes strayed to the long, lean lines of his legs as he strode across the stage to join her.

"And I object to your manners," he retorted cheerfully.

"I consider myself an excellent consultant on matters of domestic science."

He was standing right next to her, the scent of his after shave teasing her nostrils and reminding her all too vividly of what it was like to bury her nose in that intoxicating smell. Britt was in favor of his being there, Angie knew, and to object now would seem like sour grapes. She would have to concede, and the only choice was to do it gracefully. "Ladies and gentle—" Angie stopped in the middle of the word *gentlemen* when she remembered that Kyle was the only man around. "May I introduce Mr. Kyle Bennett, an entrepreneur from..." She paused and waited for him to answer.

"New York City," he stated, and looked at her eagerly. "So," he said, "what do you want me to do?"

She picked up a blender encrusted with three days' worth of food. "Here," she said flatly, handing it to him. "Clean it."

"No big deal," he shrugged, and headed over to the sink. "First, a little dishwashing detergent." He dramatically squirted a three-foot stream into the blender. "Add water, and—"

Angie shook her head, expecting him to start washing it in the sink, but to her astonishment he plunked the blender back onto its motor base.

"I read your column," he exclaimed proudly, and flicked on the machine. *"Voilà!* A self-cleaner!"

Suddenly, soap bubbles and water foamed out of control all over the counter, and Kyle jumped back in alarm.

"Try using a cover before you start it up," Angie suggested drolly, and casually placed the top on the blender.

Kyle looked startled but grinned gamely as Angie

handed him a paper towel. Their hands brushed briefly—did he run his hand across hers on purpose?—and a little shiver went through her at the contact. Her heart seemed to be jumping out of control at his powerful presence, and the solemn promise he had made to her about the inevitable intimacy of their relationship seemed to loom over her like a dark, sensual cloud. Abruptly, she turned off the blender and pushed it to the side, willing herself to stay calm. This man made her feel like a powder keg. At any second, she might explode.

"Nice try," she said to him, forcing a flippant tone. "But next time read the whole article."

"I forgot that one small detail." His eyes were sparked with some private amusement, and she knew that he didn't really care about the blender, didn't care about the demonstration at all. She faced him squarely, determined to wear him down.

"Care to go another round?" she asked coolly.

He looked to the side where Samantha was winking at him, and gave her a helpless shrug. "What's next?"

The audience waited expectantly, and Angie was once more in control as the questions started up. Apparently no one had noticed the electricity that was generating between the two people on stage, and she was determined to keep it that way. She faced her audience and took questions one at a time.

"Are there any ways in which to avoid doing dishes all the time?"

"Paper plates!" Kyle exclaimed, a finger in the air.

"Also husbands and children," Angie put in.

"What about scratches on furniture?"

"Try a little shoe polish. Just remember to match the color."

"Coffee works well, also," Kyle remarked unexpectedly.

Angie turned to him, surprised. "That's true," she admitted. "Where'd you learn that?"

"I spilled some coffee by accident in the middle of an experiment. Worked like a charm." His blue eyes faced her frankly, unraveling her composure as she stared into their clear depths. How was it possible for one man to affect her so? She wanted to strangle him and wrap her arms around him in an embrace simultaneously.

"Great moments in scientific history," she quipped, trying to ward off his spell. But it was no use. Kyle was like a magnet that demanded her response. All this was unfolding in front of a watchful audience, and she began to feel as if everything were happening in a movie, as if this whole scene weren't real.

She didn't know how much longer she could stand on the stage, handling Kyle and the audience with equal aplomb. A questioner was asking how to get stains out of a white tablecloth, and as she explained how to pour hot water directly over the stain, she saw Kyle watching her appreciatively from the side.

"Very logical," he commented when she had finished. "I'm impressed, Supermom."

"The audience applauded politely, but Angie did not believe Kyle's seeming sincerity for a moment. The appreciation in his cobalt eyes stemmed from a purely masculine source, and they were now traveling lazily over her features in the same slow, sensual way they had across her kitchen table.

She realized that she was actually trembling, but Kyle obviously had no intention of stopping. He must have something up his sleeve, and she had the distinct feeling that he was going to reveal it publicly, without giving her an escape. As the applause died down, he held up his hands and turned to her. Before she could say anything, he said swiftly, "Now I've got a question." He leaned against the counter and folded his arms. "When are you going to jump into the ring with Benny?"

Utter silence descended as Angie groped for a suitable response. One part of her wanted to ignore him, another part of her wanted to reject his offer with cold dignity, and a third part wanted to pour the leftover cake batter all over his face. The audience waited keenly for her answer.

"Go get him, Angie," someone jeered.

"No metal contraption can replace us!" another shouted. More shouts and jeers joined the uprush, until total pandemonium set in. The audience booed Kyle, but he took their taunts with absolute calm as Angie tried to cool down her fans.

When she had their attention, she seized the moment and turned to Kyle. "You still don't understand, do you, Mr. Bennett?"

Kyle gave her a cool smile. "Oh, I understand perfectly, Ms. Carpenter," he said, emphasizing the *Ms*. "You are deluding yourself. I'm offering you a chance to retire from drudgery and you refuse to take it. Are you a martyr, or is it just that you're afraid of the truth?" His eyes were pinning her with their intensity, and the hum that rippled through the crowd echoed the angry buzz in her head.

"If I accept your challenge," she said bitingly, "will you announce to the world how wrong you were after I win?"

"And if you lose?" Kyle pressed. "Will you admit the same?"

Suddenly, it dawned on her. She was trapped. If she

lost the contest to Benny, her career was finished. No one would ever take her columns seriously again, and she would become a symbol of dismal failure. And if she refused to compete, she would look like a coward, thereby proving his point. Her only choice was to compete—and to win. Kyle Bennett now held her career in his hands. She couldn't back down. She had been a fool to fall into his trap, but it was too late.

"I accept," she said with cold dignity.

The audience went wild with applause and shouts of approval, but although she tried valiantly to maintain a smile, a lump rose in her throat. Her only rational thought was that she wanted to strangle Kyle Bennett.

Samantha was the first to congratulate her as she followed Kyle off the stage. "You were great, Mom."

"Oh, I loved it, dear," Britt was raving. "And this contest! It's going to make front-page headlines all across the country."

Angie ignored both of them as she ducked behind the stage after Kyle. Before he could get any farther, she reached for his shoulder and whipped him around.

"Why are you here?" she demanded hotly. She knew that her hands were shaking, but she didn't care.

Kyle shrugged innocently and gestured off to his side. "She invited me."

Angie turned on Britt, ready to vent her anger.

"Don't look at me, sweetie," Britt objected in her breathy voice. "It's a simply *fabulous* idea, but I'm sorry to say I didn't think of it."

"I wasn't talking about Britt," Kyle interjected. He gestured toward Samantha, who shrank behind her mother in a halfhearted attempt to duck out of sight.

Everyone stared incredulously at her, and at last she

stepped forward with a philosophical sigh. "Well," she dodged, looking back and forth from one adult to the other, "don't blame me." She tugged guiltily on one fat chestnut braid and shrugged. "Pyrotechnical situations call for pyrotechnic measures."

Chapter Five

ANGIE ADJUSTED THE scarf that complemented her black suit and firmly fastened the top button. Then she caught sight of herself in the living room mirror and frowned.

This business suit is too stodgy, she thought. I'm not a corporate climber. I can wear anything I want to a meeting in Britt's office—even if Kyle Bennett *is* going to be there. Rechecking the train schedule to the city, she dashed upstairs and changed into a summery dress with a gauzy lavender and blue flower pattern. The dress was cut with a square neck and slender straps over the shoulders, and it flared gracefully well below her knees. Angie added a pair of laced-up espadrilles, two bangly bracelets and matching earrings, and a pale blue shawl. She also toned her makeup to match the softer, lighter colors and studied the effect carefully in the mirror before sauntering downstairs again.

Samantha took one look at her and whistled loudly, her eyes sparkling.

"It's too hot for a suit," Angie said defensively.

"You can't fool me," Samantha replied breezily as she headed out the door. "I know why you changed."

"Why?" Angie asked uncomfortably. Having a nine-year-old daughter could be more disconcerting than living with another adult. Samantha's perceptions were usually on target, and the concept of tact was still a developing notion to her.

Samantha stopped, turned around, and gave her mother a wide grin. "Subterfuge," she answered, as if any idiot would have known. "An underhanded plot."

This analysis bothered Angie all the way into the city. I don't need to use subterfuge to get what I want, she thought irritably. The trouble was she wasn't sure what she wanted. All she knew was that she had been feeling different ever since she met Kyle Bennett. His bold words had burned into her memory, making her want to taunt him and run from him at the same time.

But did she have to do something as obvious as wear a sexy, romantic dress?

She smiled to herself at the question. Why not? she reasoned daringly. Better to meet the enemy dressed to kill.

The effect was not wasted. "Oh, I *love* that dress," was the first thing Britt said when Angie sailed into her office. She gestured delicately at the square neckline that bared Angie's slender throat. "But don't you think it's a little—er—" Britt paused and giggled. "Inappropriate for a Supermom?" The breathiness disappeared abruptly as she issued a command. "Try and select something more homey for the contest, dear."

Angie was about to protest when two distinguished-looking gentlemen appeared. Britt promptly introduced them as Ernest Mayhew and Bertram Fellows, two lawyers from the magazine. Both men wore conservative black suits and humorless expressions, and they looked like a matched set of undertakers. They took seats off to the side, and while they all waited for the other competitor to arrive, Britt passed around a forty-page typewritten manual entitled *Supermom Versus Benny The Robot*. Angie picked it up curiously and realized that this was going to be a very long meeting indeed. And the other key player hadn't even arrived yet.

"Sorry I'm late," Kyle Bennett said, right on cue, as he breezed into the room. His tie was loose and his hair looked tousled, giving him a rakish, carefree look. "I just came from a rather long business meeting in Washington. My flight was delayed." He stopped suddenly when he noticed what Angie was wearing, and gave her a melting smile. Angie tried to look cool and dignified, but she was torn between decorum and the unexpected rush of pleasure she felt the moment Kyle entered the room. The two lawyers, as indistinguishable as Mutt and Jeff in their dark suits and rep ties, gave him perfunctory nods, and Britt invitingly patted the seat next to her.

When he caught sight of the booklet placed on the table in front of him, he laughed delightedly. "What's this?" he asked wryly. "The latest best-seller?"

"Those are the rules of the contest," Angie informed him. "You do remember the contest, don't you?"

"Oh, yes." He beamed. "I'm all ready. Do we shake hands and come out fighting?"

"Not just yet, sweetie," Britt said and, after introducing Bert and Ernie, got down to business. "Page one, everyone," she said seriously. "The object of the contest..." She waited for everyone's complete attention and then continued. "The object of this contest is to see if a robot can outperform a homemaker in a controlled environment. The equipment is as follows."

Angie looked down at the list and her eyes widened in surprise. They were each to be supplied with separate, identical houses, side by side, in the town of Wyandanch, a small community on Long Island.

"Looks like we'll be neighbors," Kyle whispered confidentially, making her jump.

Angie was stunned. "You expect us to move? To live in these houses for the duration?"

Britt gave her a chilly smile. "Well, of course, dear. How else can we *monitor* the results? Besides," she went on in honeyed tones, "I think you'll like some of the fringe benefits." She turned a page and everyone followed suit. "Each house will be furnished with identical sets of furniture and equipment as well as outdoor trash cans and cars."

"Cars?" Angie repeated incredulously.

"Brand-new Ford Escorts," Fellows confirmed in a flinty lawyer's voice, producing twin sets of keys. "It wouldn't be completely fair if you used different kinds of automobiles. And we want to be sure that a car won't break down during the course of the contest. That would give an unfair disadvantage."

Angie and Kyle exchanged brief, awed glances. Clearly, this contest was turning out to be far more serious and demanding than either one of them had anticipated. The judges seemed to have thought of everything. Chastened, they both looked down at their booklets as Britt continued.

"The contest will be judged by Mr. Fellows and Mr. Mayhew—these two lovely gentlemen," she indicated, pointing a long pink fingernail at them. "They will have access to your homes from the time you wake up until after dinner."

"What happens after dinner?" Kyle asked cautiously. "We turn into pumpkins?"

"It's free time," Mayhew explained tonelessly. "You may do whatever you like."

Kyle immediately gave Angie a wickedly suggestive grin, and she looked away. But it was difficult not to react humorously to the utter sobriety with which the contest was being put together.

"Ahhemm." Britt cleared her throat and glared at them. "The contest is to be three days long and will consist of three major parts." They all turned the pages of the booklet in unison. "Part one is general cleaning. You'll be graded on a scale of one to a hundred."

Angie read along with everyone else. It was a simple enough contest. They were to move into prearranged messes with manufactured dirt. All they had to do was clean them up.

"Each unit will be prestained with specific dirt natural to that particular area of the house," Britt read aloud, and Angie found herself stifling a laugh. It all seemed so silly when put in this light. She couldn't believe how much trouble they had gone to just to set up this contest. It was turning into full-scale war, complete with weapons and machinery.

"For example," Britt was continuing earnestly, "you'll find kitchen floors with waxy yellow buildup, stains on carpets, walls, and furniture, and a dirty ring around the tub."

"What, no ring around the collar?" Kyle quipped.

"You've got every other cliché."

Angie did laugh this time, but Britt remained unfazed. "We're just coming to that," she informed him calmly, effectively squelching his mirth. "The second part of the contest is general day-to-day living. This includes shopping for food, cooking, washing dishes and laundry, as well as taking out the garbage."

Angie couldn't restrain her own curiosity. "Benny can do all that?"

"And more," Kyle answered promptly. "While you're killing yourself trying to clean that house, I'll be relaxing with a good book or just lounging on the beach."

Angie shot him a competitive glance. "Is that so, Mr. Clean? Well, don't be so sure. I may just join you."

Kyle pretended to ponder that idea for a moment. Then his face lit up in an inviting grin. "It's a date," he concluded. "I hope you can make it."

Angie was instantly on guard, but Britt was turning the page again, gearing up for something that was obviously of keen interest to her. She favored everyone with a secretive smile and gushed, "Now, this last part is going to be *really* fun." She paused dramatically. "We call it Revenge."

"Revenge?" Angie uncrossed her sleek legs and sat up. "What kind?"

"Well," Britt said coyly, "let's just say that you'll be given the opportunity to do unto Mr. Bennett as he will do unto you."

Angie frowned. "I still don't understand."

"Neither do I," Kyle spoke up. They looked at each other nervously. Britt didn't seem to realize it, but her attitude was only serving to throw the two competitors together. She also didn't know that this presented extra problems for Angie, who was finding it necessary to keep Kyle at arm's length. But this was something they hadn't expected. "It sounds intriguing," Kyle said hopefully in response to Britt's sly wink. "What is it?"

But Britt shook her head, the saccharine overtones disappearing. "Sorry, but that's a surprise."

"I don't like surprises," Angie said darkly. "The last surprise I had resulted in my being here today."

Britt reached over and patted her hand in a consoling manner. "Don't worry so much. You'll both have a good time. I *promise*."

"Well, are there at least any rules to the last part?" Kyle pursued.

"Yes," Angie asked, genuinely worried. "Can't you give us a little hint?"

"You want a *hint?*" Britt looked doubtfully at the two lawyers, who shrugged obligingly. "Well, let's see..." There was a momentary silence as she thought it over, and then her face broke into a sly grin. "In this last part of the contest..." she began, searching for the right words, "...*anything goes*." She looked at Bert and Ernie for confirmation, and they nodded together like two marionettes on the same string. No one spoke for a moment. Angie stole a glance at Kyle, who seemed to be contemplating this intently. He caught her stare and looked up.

"Penny for your thoughts?" he asked amiably.

"Sorry," she said warily. "My thoughts don't come that cheap."

"Would either of you like to know what the prize is?" Britt broke in coolly.

"Prize?" they asked in unison.

Again Britt turned to the next page and Angie and

Kyle followed suit. As Angie read the details, her eyes lit up in amazement.

"Now, this is worth fighting for," she said. "Oh, Samantha will love this."

"A two-week, all-expenses-paid trip to Hawaii," Kyle read excitedly. He looked up at Britt. "Thank you," he said warmly. "I can certainly use a vacation."

"So can I," Angie jumped in heatedly. "So can I."

"Well, then," Britt spoke up. "I suggest we read through the rest of the details of the contest. If you have any questions, let's clear them up before you leave this room."

Three hours later, thoroughly drained, Angie and Kyle found themselves riding the same elevator down to the street. Whatever antagonism had been hovering between them was now banished by the tedium they had just shared, and by the humorless attitude toward the contest that had been projected by the usually ebullient Britt.

"What would you say to a late afternoon lunch?" Kyle asked affably as they stepped from the elevator and walked out of the building to the crowded street.

The sun was warm and inviting on Angie's face, and throwing caution to the four winds, she nodded. "If you don't mind fraternizing with the enemy?" she teased.

Kyle laughed heartily and hailed the first cab that came along. A few seconds later they were heading downtown, both totally frazzled, but definitely on the same wavelength. "Fifth Avenue and Eighth Street," Kyle said to the driver.

"Fifth and Eighth?" Angie repeated. "What restaurant is there?"

"Restaurant?" Kyle looked at her with mock innocence. "Who said anything about a restaurant? All I promised was a late afternoon lunch. What better place to have it than at my apartment?"

Angie leaned back, too exhausted to argue. "Of course," she said, slapping her forehead. "You plan on plying me with liquor. Or do you simply want me to see your etchings?"

"Just consider it a friendly handshake before the starting gun goes off," he suggested dryly.

"Subterfuge," she mumbled knowingly. "I've been hoodwinked."

"I wouldn't call it that. Not yet, anyway."

"Oh?" She folded her arms and looked at him sternly. "Then what exactly would you call it?"

"I call it lunch," he said with a straight face, refusing to rise to the bait.

She delicately lifted an eyebrow. "You have nothing else in mind?"

His eyes glinted suddenly, and the corners of his mouth seemed to be resisting a smile. "In the immortal words of Britt Shapiro Whittaker," he said cunningly, "anything goes."

What he didn't realize, Angie thought later, was that the phrase should have been directed more to how Kyle Bennett lived his life than to what was destined to happen between herself and him. From the outside, Kyle's building was a typical modern apartment complex, but the gracious if sterile lobby and the smooth elevator ride were only a front. From the moment they entered his apartment, Angie knew exactly why he had been so insistent to pursue this contest. She wanted to burst out laughing, but she kept her composure for fear of being rude, and stood helplessly in the doorway, desperately containing her glee.

Kyle disappeared briefly into the kitchen, and Angie could hear him directing Benny to make two hero sandwiches. It was odd to know he was talking to a robot, and she wondered if the rest of his apartment would be this disconcerting.

"Lunch will be ready in fifteen minutes," he announced as he reappeared. "It's all set."

"You've got to be kidding!" she managed to blurt out.

"Kidding?" he asked. "No, don't worry. Benny is quite reliable."

"I wasn't talking about that," she answered, looking around the room. "I was talking about this *place*."

In a living room the size of a football field, a space that looked as if it could easily entertain the New York Jets plus the Mormon Tabernacle Choir, stood exactly four pieces of furniture. And that was only if you used the word *furniture* in the broadest sense.

"Is this for real?" Angie persisted, fearing a practical joke.

She made her way in slowly as her eyes scanned the room like a movie camera. She gazed out the huge curtainless windows at the lower skyline of New York and then drew her eyes back to the nonview inside. There was one large reclining chair in the center of the enormous room. A lamp stood behind it, and what appeared to be a coffee table sat in front of it. At least it had a coffee mug on it. To Angie, it looked as if someone had chopped down a tree, shellacked it, and then dropped it off in Kyle's living room as an afterthought.

"That's a real oak stump," Kyle said, noticing her perplexity. "You like it?"

Actually, it had a nice, rustic look to it. But it looked so ridiculous sitting there all by itself. It could have used a sofa and a few more chairs around it to make it look less lonely.

"Uh—well, it's very nice," Angie stuttered. She didn't

quite know how she had gotten herself into this situation—alone with Kyle in his apartment. It was difficult to feel comfortable here; the place was too startling to be welcoming. And Kyle's casual, easy manner was an abrupt turnaround from the brazen way he had talked to her in her kitchen.

But as she looked around his odd domain, something occurred to her. Any lamebrain could clean a living room as barren as this one—even a robot.

"There's no competition here," she said. "I'm afraid Benny will be in for quite a shock. Suburban homes can get quite cluttered and confusing, you know." She scanned the room with new eagerness. On the far wall across from the window was a huge ten-foot-square painting of a red circle. Just one red circle in the middle of a white blank.

"That's an original Kenneth Noland," Kyle informed her proudly. "Do you like modern art?"

"Not this kind," she answered honestly. "I won't go so far as to say that Samantha could have painted this, but it's not really something I'd care to hang in my living room." Moving over to the window, she looked down at what appeared to be two black leather seats in amorphous shapes. After a moment's deliberation, she carefully tried sitting on one as an experiment. All at once she began to feel that she was being swallowed alive as her body sank and sank into the depths. In no time at all the thing gently changed shape to fit the contours of her body.

Kyle smiled knowingly. "I love to relax in those," he said. "My partner invented them. He calls them blobs."

"An appropriate name," Angie said, attempting to remove herself from the clutches of the seat. It wasn't easy. She leaned all the way back to get enough momentum and then tried to spring up, but she found she was trapped helplessly in the depths of the chair. Kyle saw her predicament and obligingly offered his hand. She gripped it firmly and tried again, this time succeeding in leaping free. Stumbling forward, she practically fell into Kyle's arms. "Oh! Excuse me," she stammered, backing away immediately. The last thing she wanted was to give him ideas. He already had enough of his own.

Kyle watched her confusion calmly, as if waiting for her to relax before making his move. "Come on," he said, taking her hand. "I'll show you the rest of the apartment."

He led her down the hall and stopped as he opened a door and gestured her inside. "I should have known," she couldn't help saying as she stepped in. This room was cluttered but organized, filled with a desk, a swivel chair, a sophisticated computer, and a drafting table littered with different types of tools. There were neat stacks of papers, a small telescope, a set of Bunsen burners, and sets of blueprints scattered over the various surfaces, and the walls were covered with framed diplomas and lists of things to be done. Angie caught the names Harvard and MIT, and swallowed back her jumpiness. Clearly, Kyle Bennett was some sort of genius.

But he was the world's worst decorator. As they left the workroom and entered the bedroom, she was not surprised to see a platform bed with starched white sheets and a plain khaki blanket, and a small file cabinet next to it that served as a nightstand. That was all.

Angie gingerly touched the mattress, expecting it to be rock-hard. Instead, it undulated gently. "A water bed?" she asked, amazed.

"A special gelatin compound," Kyle explained. "It molds and folds to the exact contours of the body."

"Invented, no doubt, by the same person who created the blob chair," she guessed. "Am I right?"

"You'd like Alpha," Kyle confirmed eagerly. He punched the mattress with his palm, making it roll and sway.

"Alpha?" she repeated dubiously. "Your friend's name is Alpha?"

"Actually, it's Alan Phizer, but he likes to be called Alpha. It makes him feel like a mad scientist."

"That's the pot calling the kettle," Angie mumbled.

Kyle was watching her knowingly. "Don't be so nervous, Angie."

"Nervous about what?" she asked.

"And don't look at me with that oh-so-innocent expression. Why don't you sit down?" he suggested hospitably. "I think we have a lot to talk about."

"Like what?" she asked warily.

"Like why you really agreed to this contest. Like why a rapport has sprung up between us that is so irresistible I can't think about anything else. Like where you've been all my life, and why you married what's-his-name." He paused. "And why you got divorced."

Angie took a deep breath, unconsciously clutching her hands together like a young girl singing in a church choir. "The answer to the first question is that you tricked me into it."

"Wrong," he said at once. "You were determined not to get into this. You could have weaseled out of it. Granted, I am extremely clever"— he ignored her pointed glare —"but I'm sure you could have thought of a way."

"Well," she floundered, "I guess I thought I had something to prove."

"Now we're getting somewhere." He nodded. "You think you have to prove that you're invincible. That you don't need anyone. That you can manage to stumble through life entirely by yourself."

"Well, I wouldn't put it quite that way."

"I would." He advanced toward her, backing her toward the bed. "You think you can run a house without any help, and I'm sure you're right. But what you won't admit is that you can't get through life without a man by your side."

"That's an outrageous statement!" she cried, truly angry. "That is positively medieval!"

"I know." He grinned, unrepentant. "And you're missing my point. You need someone, Angie. You're this cool, perfect paragon going through life with your elbows out. No one can touch you." His smile vanished, and his blue eyes bored into hers. "But I will," he vowed. "I will because I can sense the volcano underneath the cool front." He walked forward again, and she bumped against the bed and plunked down. The pliant mattress dipped and undulated beneath her.

Kyle sat down next to her and took her hand. She couldn't help flinching a little at the contact. Kyle's touch was charged with electricity, but he seemed so gentle now that she let her hand rest in his. "Would you like to answer my other questions?" he asked softly. "Like where you've been all my life?"

Angie smiled a little, and looked down. "I'm sure a brainy type like you can come up with something more original than that."

"Not really. I want to know all about you."

"Why?" she asked, suddenly suspicious. "You're my opponent, remember? Why should I give you any ammunition?"

He held up his hands in self-defense. "You don't have to tell me anything you don't want to. And in exchange, I'll tell you anything you want to know about me." He extended a hand. "Deal?"

She smiled slowly. "Deal." They shook hands gravely, and he kept her hand imprisoned in his once again. "I'm not so mysterious," she began, feeling self-conscious. "I grew up on Long Island, had a normal childhood, and married young."

"But it didn't last," he observed quietly.

She sighed. "No."

There was a pause, and then he asked, "What happened?"

Angie had talked about her divorce to very few people, but for some reason she didn't mind telling Kyle about it. "Nothing happened," she began tentatively. "And I mean nothing. Clark was a wonderful provider—he still is. But he worked constantly and seemed more married to his work than he was to me. He left the house at six-thirty in the morning and didn't come home until seven or eight at night. There were whole weeks when Samantha didn't see him at all."

Angie looked out the window, remembering. "One Sunday morning we looked at each other across the breakfast table and I realized that we hadn't had a real conversation in months. We didn't say a word about it, but on that day we both knew that it was over. It wasn't that it had come to an end. It was that it never really began. When Clark moved out, Samantha and I were as alone as we had always been."

Kyle was watching her steadily during this recital, his face open and waiting for her to finish. "After that it was easy." She shrugged. She hesitated suddenly, her hands unconsciously playing with the cover on the bed. What she had just said wasn't really true. She looked back at that period in her life and saw only a long, dull stretch of gray.

"Easy?" Kyle said softly, seeing the change in her face. "I doubt that very much."

"Am I that transparent?" She shook her head ruefully. "I guess I am." Her voice was barely above a whisper. "I had wanted a real home, a family, and suddenly everything was upside down. I thought my life was mapped out for me when I got married, and there I was, a divorcée. The funny part was that my life with Clark had never felt like a real marriage. So I was divorced without ever having been married."

Tears sprang to her eyes, and she dabbed at them quickly with her free hand. "No matter what happens, I will never, ever again commit myself to a man who is more in love with his work than with his family," she vowed in a fierce whisper. She looked up at Kyle fearfully, wondering if she had gone too far. Did he think she was talking about him? She looked down and bit her lip. Kyle was obviously in love with his work, but he was also in ardent pursuit of her. And Samantha was crazy about him. It was too soon to tell where his priorities would fall. "I'm being silly," she said quickly, trying to dismiss her conflicting doubts.

"No, you're not," he said urgently, pressing her hand.

This confused her even more. Was he trying to tell her that she was right in her convictions, or right to have doubts about him? She looked up at him and saw them suddenly as they were—a man and a woman sitting together on a bed, holding hands. She tried to stand up, but Kyle followed her motion and pulled her toward him. "Where are you going?" he asked. She turned quickly and bumped directly into him. The contact was swift and fierce, and suddenly the question they had been avoiding hung before them like a bright moon in a dark night. Everything had been leading toward this moment, and Kyle had been right about one thing. She was going to have to face up to the current running between them.

"I like you, Kyle," she said bravely, looking him straight in the eye. "You're a little mad, but I like that."

His face changed subtly, vulnerability cutting through the smooth veneer. "You're so . . . clear-eyed and serene and fresh," he said with a sudden candor that sent a tingle through her blood. "And I'm not . . . a normal person," he added, surprising her beyond words.

"You're a free spirit, that's all," she said feelingly, looking up at him with new courage. "I—I admire that."

Suddenly there was nothing left to say. Angie looked up at Kyle, feeling small and lost for a second before he drew her reassuringly close. He took her head in his hands and gazed down at her, his eyes becoming a rich, clear blue that held her spellbound. His face was blossoming with tenderness, showing her a side of him that had remained deeply hidden until now. She was deeply moved and fluttering with anticipation.

When he kissed her, she closed her eyes in breathless expectancy, wanting him to master her and yet needing to know that he was in her power as well. Their tongues met in perfect harmony, swirling and dancing together until they were both dizzy with longing.

The kiss lasted for a small eternity, and when it finally ended, her eyes were still languorously closed.

"Trust me, Angie," he whispered against her disheveled hair. "I can't explain it, but I swear you'll never regret it."

He kissed her again, but this time he was not gentle or subtle. He crushed her to him, as if wanting to meld her body into his. His hands ran possessively over her body, relishing her curves and creating a stream of fire that licked at every nerve ending. Angie sank back on the bed, her eyes half open as she watched him lower the straps of her dress. Then her eyes closed again as he kissed her bare shoulders and inched the dress down slowly to reveal the tops of her breasts.

She didn't know why, but everything seemed so easy, so natural, with Kyle. They were supposed to compete in a contest, and yet, strangely, she felt as if they were friends . . . no, more than friends. Passion rose gracefully within her, like smoke weaving upward from a fire. Her hands played with his thick, wavy hair as his head moved down and his hands pushed the cotton fabric over the tender peaks of her breasts. They were a delicate shade of pink and he gazed at them in wonder. "Lovely," he said huskily. "Look how lovely you are." Angie murmured an incoherent response, moaning at the assault of pleasure as he carefully took one delicate tip in his mouth.

"Oh, Kyle," she breathed, astounded at the depth of her reaction. It was as if they were connected on the same electrical current, both charged on the same wavelength to the same stunning heights.

She gasped slightly as he nipped gently, and was surprised and strangely awed to realize that his hands were trembling. Burrowing even more deeply into the pleasure as he moved to her other breast, she became aware of his ragged breathing and rejoiced in her feminine power.

Lifting his head and pinning her with his liquid blue gaze, he murmured, "You are all woman, Angie. I knew that the first time I saw you." He sat up and quickly unbuttoned his shirt, letting the two halves hang open as he bent down to gather her close. She felt the shock of her silky skin against the hard planes of his chest, and instinctively they wrapped their arms around each other to heighten the sensation. He drew back and kissed her briefly, teasing her with his tongue until she clasped his head in her hands and made him sit still for a long, lush exchange. Spiraling together in fiery bliss, Angie felt as if they were completely protected in a world that existed only for them. Nothing could mar this moment.

But something did. From the cold reality of the real world, Benny trundled in with a tray of sandwiches, his lights blinking busily. Angie jumped up and pulled the covers over her body, irrationally embarrassed to be caught half-naked, albeit by a robot. Benny actually seemed to be staring at her disapprovingly, and suddenly everything felt all wrong.

"Don't mind him," Kyle whispered, easing her back on the bed.

She sat up again insistently. "No, Kyle. This is just too crazy. And too soon." His eyes flickered for a moment and then hardened, but he said nothing. Benny stood motionless, his mysterious lights still blinking. "I'm not ready for this," she continued firmly, looking at the robot. "Don't you see that this is just not the right place—or the right time?"

"I told you I wouldn't rush you, Angie, and I meant it," he said. His voice was quiet, but there was an undertone of command. "But you and I are going to be lovers, and you may as well get used to that idea. Because when you're ready, I'll be waiting."

Chapter Six

THE DOORBELL RANG the next morning during breakfast.

"I'll get it," Samantha said, and ran from the kitchen table leaving her cereal half eaten. Angie could hear her opening the door, and then there was total silence.

"Who is it, Samantha?" she called. A little jump of anticipation went through her because she had the irrational feeling that it was Kyle. She caught herself hoping that it was and stifled a groan of dismay. The man always managed to affect her, no matter what she was doing.

But it wasn't Kyle. As she waited, a young man in top hat and tails suddenly appeared. An accordion was strapped around his shoulders, and he carried a huge bouquet of roses.

"Angie Carpenter?" She nodded, speechless.

"These are for you," he said, handing her the flowers. She placed them in a bowl by the sink and took the small envelope that was attached. Inside was a ticket to an opening at the Guggenheim Museum. "Kenneth Noland," she read with amusement. "A retrospective." She smiled and shook her head. "He couldn't just ask me to a movie?"

The musician flashed an entertainer's grin. "And now for my musical message," he announced with a flourish.

"Wow, a singing telegram!" Samantha said, settling down to watch. "Neato."

The young man bowed gallantly, cleared his throat, and went into the introduction to his song, which Angie recognized as being from *My Fair Lady*.

"'On the Street Where You Live,' right?"

"Music by Lerner and Loewe," he added. "But the lyrics are by Mr. Kyle Bennett."

"This is really neat," Samantha said, giggling.

"Shhhh," Angie quieted her. "Let's listen."

Sure enough, the tune was the same, but the lyrics—the lyrics were truly original. The messenger had the air of a true showman, with a booming Broadway voice to match.

"I have always walked
city streets before,
Suburban living always sounded
like a crashing bore.
All at once will I
to the suburbs fly,
To compete on the street where you live!
I find you sublime
and Samantha's fine,
And the meeting that we had
left me so well inclined.

But you left so soon,
running from my room,
Leaving me all alone without you.
And ohhhhh, the towering feeling
as I thought of nothing but you.
The overpowering feeling
when I realized there is something I must do.
So I send this song
knowing soon you'll be
Right next door to good old Benny
and yours truly—me.
But until that time
It-t-t-t-t would be a crime,
knowing you'll be on the street where I live!"

The song ended as the young man gave another bow, this time with a considerable flourish.

This bravura performance was met with a dead silence, broken at last by the sound of sparse but enthusiastic applause from Samantha.

"Nifty," she commented warmly. "Very ingenious."

Angie shot her a look. "Uh, yes, that was—truly unique," she managed to say. She was too stunned to say much more. "Uh, Samantha, please show the young man out. And thank you."

He bowed cordially and left as quickly as he had come. Angie examined the ticket in her hand with trepidation.

"It's for next Sunday afternoon," Samantha said with interest as she looked over her mother's shoulder. "That's the day before the contest is to begin."

"So it is," Angie said, growing suspicious of such a tactic. "So it is." She continued to ponder it, still not sure what to make of it. "He could have asked me to a movie or a Broadway show," she mused. "But a modern art exhibit? I *hate* modern art. And he *knows* I do."

"Then why did he invite you to a museum?" Samantha asked.

But Angie wasn't going to answer that one. It was obvious, she realized. He was testing her to see if she would show up. He knew she didn't like Kenneth Noland; the only motive for her to come was to see Kyle Bennett ... if she came. "How clever," she murmured to herself. She turned to a puzzled Samantha and smiled. "Ingenious."

A week later, Angie found herself in front of the Guggenheim Museum on Fifth Avenue, dressed in a black-and-white geometric-print dress. She had chosen the dress deliberately to match the stark lines of the exhibit; she wondered if anyone would catch her wit.

KENNETH NOLAND, A RETROSPECTIVE, a large sign just inside the door read. She headed past it and into the main rotunda of the gallery, where a small chamber orchestra was playing a quartet by some unknown composer. Although she had no idea what she was listening to, the music helped to soothe her nerves. Stepping quietly to one side, she looked carefully around the gallery, hoping to find Kyle as soon as possible. She had never called to confirm that she would meet him, had not definitely decided to come, in fact, until late last night. Now she was curious to see if he would be relieved to see her, or if he would have the nerve to gloat.

Her eyes were drawn round and round as they followed the circular walkway that spiraled up and up to the ceiling. Hundreds of people sipped champagne and nibbled caviar as they strolled casually from one painting to the next along the slanting passage. The men were all dressed in black tie, and the women, sporting designer originals in bright colors, paraded around like peacocks. Penguins and peacocks, Angie quipped to herself. It was quite a show.

If Kyle was here, she reasoned, he was probably making his way up and around the spiraling gallery. But one penguin was starting to look pretty much like the next to her, and she knew that she would have to ferret out Mr. Kyle Bennett herself.

She began the ascent slowly, passing paintings that consisted of neat circles and lines, and had just made it safely around the bend when she saw Kyle standing in front of one of the circular paintings. He carried the formal clothing with elegant ease, and for a moment she forgot all about her wariness.

"Unbelievable," she overheard him say to himself as well as to a couple who stood sipping champagne next to him. "I never tire of the way he expresses the relationship between circle and square."

"Are you kidding?" she asked bluntly, suddenly determined to needle him. "Any child could have painted that."

Kyle turned quickly, ready to voice a retort, but he took one look at Angie and the words died in his throat. His laser-blue eyes swept admiringly over the sleek curves of her dress, pausing to linger on the subtle curve of shoulder line and the teasing ruffle that bordered the hem.

"Lord, Angie, you look beautiful," he breathed softly.

He couldn't seem to stop staring at her, and she felt a warm flush rising up from deep within her. It was as if he had focused a spotlight on her and refused to take it off. "You're embarrassing me, Kyle. I'm not a painting, you know." The effect of his stare was disturbing. He was undressing her with his eyes and yet she seemed to exist only for him. She felt almost naked standing there under his scrutiny, but no one else could see her except Kyle. Suddenly, she felt wanton and beautiful and free, a spontaneous sensuality mushrooming inside of her.

The electricity between them heightened as Kyle drew one strong arm around her waist and gave her a gentle but powerful kiss that caused her senses to reel for a delicious second. "I've been waiting for you," he said huskily, causing a glimmer of triumph to shine in her eyes. "I'm so glad you came. It was a wonderful idea." His eyes swept over her again, and he shook his head as if to ward off her spell. "You have no idea what you're doing to me, do you?"

Angie caught her breath as another strong tingle shivered through her. If he was going to shower her with this kind of attention, she wasn't going to stop him. He had taunted her by saying he wasn't going to court her, but that's exactly what he was doing.

"Shall we look around the exhibit?" she suggested.

"Of course," Kyle agreed. "When I get finished with you, you'll be a convert."

They spent the better part of the afternoon walking around the museum hand in hand, and although Kyle failed to convert Angie to the wonders of circles and lines, they found a new rapport as they aired their differences. Angie found herself more interested in Kyle than his subject matter. He was dynamic and articulate in his enthusiasm, and his mental agility was stimulating in a way she had never before experienced. She had thought that she wouldn't be able to keep up with him, but his excitement was catching. By the time they reached the last level of the museum, they were engaged in a friendly but heated discussion, and Angie was exhilarated to find that she was more than holding her own.

"Whew!" she said when they came to the end. "Time out!" Kyle nodded in agreement and gave her a brief but potent kiss. Angie was startled but not really surprised. The tension had been slowly building between them, and they both knew where it was leading. "Shall we go?" she whispered.

Again he nodded. "Let's go back to my apartment and finish the other discussion we began a week ago." His tone was husky and persuasive, but she shook her head.

"I can't," she said honestly. "Samantha is expecting me for dinner and—"

"Sounds great," he said at once. He took her by the arm and headed for the door. "Let's get going. I'll drive you home."

"But—"

"I'm inviting myself for dinner," he explained with his usual self-assurance. "I want a home-cooked meal prepared by a Supermom."

Angie grinned reluctantly. "The night before the contest starts?" she protested. "Are you planning on stealing my trade secrets?"

"Oh, no," he said loftily, "I don't need them. This is strictly a social evening."

"I see," she said levelly, and she did. Kyle's pursuit of her was double-edged—first the contest and now this—and he wasn't going to let one motive get in the way of the other. Her daughter was going to be there for dinner, but Samantha had been invited to a pajama party at a friend's house, which meant that Angie and Kyle would be left quite alone for the better part of the evening. Of course, Kyle didn't know that.

The drive to Long Island was companionably quiet. The calm before the storm, Angie thought to herself. But the real storm came during dinner.

Samantha was delighted to have Kyle over, welcoming him with gushing hospitality. While Angie prepared the meal, Kyle and Samantha retreated to Samantha's room, where he was given a lecture on the latest nine-year-old toys and hobbies.

"Neato," Kyle said with a straight face as he and Samantha bounded into the dining room. "I just had a great time playing with Mr. Potato Head. Up you go." He lifted Samantha into the air and deposited her in a seat. Angie took the one opposite her daughter and Kyle sat at the head of the table. As Angie began dishing out orange and grapefruit sections, Samantha announced, "I showed Kyle my solar-system drawing. Only I think I made Jupiter too small, right, Kyle?"

"Don't worry about it," Kyle assured her. "You'd need a whole other piece of oaktag just to get Jupiter on there." Samantha looked puzzled, and Kyle reached for a whole grapefruit from a bowl and and tossed it up in the air a few times. "Jupiter," he pronounced. "Pass those peas over here, please."

Angie hesitated, but Samantha got right into the act and pushed the bowl of peas and carrots over to him.

Kyle picked up one pea and tossed it in his other hand alongside Jupiter. "This pea is the earth." He looked around for a third object, and chose a knife. "The knife is a spaceship, and it has to get away from the earth's gravitational field. Once free, it can head for Jupiter,

Anything Goes 91

or use Jupiter's gravitational field to increase its speed until—" Suddenly, his hand miscalculated the distance, and the knife dropped into the mashed potatoes. "Whoops, my spaceship crashed into a crater on the moon."

Samantha giggled uproariously and Angie couldn't help laughing.

"Wait, there's more," Kyle said, holding up a hand. "Although the grapefruit is heavier than the knife or the pea, the speed is not increased because of the mass."

"What are you talking about?" Angie asked. Samantha looked equally puzzled, and turned to him plaintively.

"Galileo and the Leaning Tower of Pisa," Kyle explained.

"Leaning tower of Pizza!" Samantha hooted.

"Okay," he said affably. "Now watch." Kyle picked up the grapefruit and took a pea up in his hand. To Angie's consternation, he then stood up on his chair, balancing precariously as he tried to make his point.

"What are you doing?" she cried. "Come down from there. You'll ruin the finish."

Kyle gave her a mischievous grin. "Don't be a drag, Angie. Any respectable Supermom knows how to fix a little thing like that." He thought for a moment. "Shoe polish, right?"

She couldn't resist his antics. "And coffee," she acknowledged with a nod.

Assured that he had their undivided attention, he announced, "I am now going to drop both of these objects at the same time." He turned to Samantha and winked. "Now, which will hit the ground first? The grapefruit or the pea?"

"The grapefruit!" Samantha cried at once. Angie said nothing, watching Kyle's performance as he charmed and educated her daughter. She remembered the basic concept he was demonstrating from eighth-grade science, but she had never seen it proven so effectively.

"You think so?" Kyle asked. "Let's see." At that instant, he let go of both the pea and the grapefruit. They hit the ground at exactly the same time.

"Look at that," Samantha observed with interest. "It works."

"Of course it works," Kyle beamed, hopping down from the chair. "End of lesson. Now, would you give me back the grapefruit and a knife and lots of planets?"

"Planets?" Samantha asked as she handed him the grapefruit.

"I mean the peas."

Angie grew worried. "What exactly are you planning, Kyle? I don't think—"

"I'm merely planning dinner," he said innocently, dishing a large helping of peas onto his plate. "Let's eat."

"That was some demonstration you gave us," Angie said after they had driven Samantha to her friend's house. "My daughter is very impressed with you."

Kyle downshifted as they approached Angie's street and gave her a sidelong grin. "And I'm impressed with her. Did you know that she has collected over eight hundred and fifty bottle caps and has a collection of every record Michael Jackson ever made since he was born?"

"Of course I know it. I've spent many a night listening to them."

"But you love it, don't you?" He wasn't merely confirming the obvious, he was really asking.

Angie looked at him thoughtfully. "Yes," she said slowly, "I do. Having a child changes your perspective."

He glanced at her with a strange kind of admiration that she didn't quite understand. Kyle wasn't really as changeable as she had first thought. It was that he was utterly brilliant in some areas, but completely naive in others. Education is a multifaceted process, she realized. She knew a lot about life that Kyle was clearly only just starting to learn.

They pulled into her driveway, and Kyle turned off the motor. Silence fell abruptly between them. The sun was almost down, and the gentle glow seemed to cast a peaceful spell on the quiet street. Angie felt shy suddenly, but she knew the feeling wouldn't last long. The end of the evening was inevitable. She knew that now. She just didn't know how they were going to move smoothly from the front seat of the car to—to the night of unleashed passion that rose invitingly before them.

"Would—would you like a brandy?" she asked hesitantly.

She glanced at him uncertainly and was gratified to see that he looked as jittery as she felt. They left the car and went into the house, soothingly quiet now that Samantha was gone. Angie's heart was beating rapidly with anticipation, wondering what to expect. She poured two large snifters of cognac and handed one to Kyle. They sat down in the living room and looked at each other across the empty space, smiling tentatively in the silence.

"Well," she said, "right now I'd like a nice, crackling fire. Unfortunately, it's June."

Kyle didn't laugh. "And right now I'd like to make passionate love to you. Fortunately, we're alone."

The glass teetered in Angie's hand and she put it down hastily. "Kyle..." she whispered, her eyes filled with longing.

He came to her and took both of her hands in his. He picked them up and kissed each one, sending little darts of longing through her. She tried to look down, but he took her chin and held it firmly as he gazed down at her. His face was all lines and planes, shadowed deeply so that only his eyes were prominent. They glowed fiercely beneath the unruly shock of dark hair, and when his face descended, Angie closed her eyes in anticipation. He kissed her once, slowly and provocatively, teasing her tongue with his until she responded, and then pulling back. "There's still a lot in you that needs to emerge, Angie."

"Like what?" she whispered, her eyes veiled.

He evaded a direct answer as he traced a delicate line with one finger from her cheek to her ear and then down to her chin. "So much," he murmured sensuously. "But it needs to be awakened slowly... with utmost tenderness and care. You're brimming with life, Angie, and I don't think you know what a magnificent woman you are." The rest of his answer was lost in the kiss that followed as they both became lost in the swirling, honeyed warmth. Angie clung to him fiercely, not realizing how much she needed his touch, and he responded at once.

Angie surprised herself by taking Kyle firmly by the hand and leading him down the hall to the bedroom. She didn't care about anything at this moment except the fire that had been stoking between them.

She stopped and looked up at him bravely. "It—it's been a long time for me, Kyle."

His face became pliant and tender as his eyes met hers. "Look at it this way," he said softly. "It's the first time for both of us—together."

She smiled shyly, and her eyes glowed as their lips met. The first kiss was slow as they found their rhythm and sank into the mood. But passion quickly enveloped them, and the enormity of what was about to happen between them made them starry-eyed and yet reckless. Somehow they knew without saying it that they were about to cross a bridge from distance to intimacy. And they knew they would never be able to go back.

Kyle slipped the black-and-white dress from her body, letting it rustle to the floor. She was wearing a full, lacy black slip underneath, and his eyes narrowed appreciatively as he looked at her silk-clad form. Angie's head fell back and she gasped suddenly as he ran his hands lightly down the sides of her body, letting his thumbs flick lightly over the tips of her breasts.

"Oh, Kyle," she murmured brokenly, and tears sprang unbidden to her eyes.

"Yes, I'm here, love," he whispered, sensuously molding her hips. "Just let me."

His hands slipped sinuously beneath the black slip, hiking it up around her hips as he drew dizzying circles around her backside and down the supple contours of her thighs.

Angie opened her eyes for a moment and saw the dazzling white of his formal shirt against the velvety blackness of the night. The stars outside the window were embedded in the inky blue sky, and she felt that she and Kyle were encased in their own special haven, away from the cares of the outside world. Kyle lifted the black slip up and over her head, pausing to help it over her taut, firm breasts. His hands were trembling, but his eyes were shining with intensity.

Angie stepped out of her shoes and her black-toned stockings and stood naked before him. She felt lustrous and free and proud all at the same time. Stepping forward boldly, she undid the clasps of his shirt and ran her nails lightly down his flat, hard chest. "Oh, Angie," he groaned, "you're a witch. You don't know what you do to me." He tore off the rest of his clothes and held her, obviously relishing the feel of softness against muscle, silk against strength.

Dropping warm, sensual kisses down the length of her slender neck and onto her graceful shoulders, he kneaded her rounded backside in both his hands. His breathing was ragged, and Angie realized with a wild kind of joy how very much he desired her. Never had she felt so dominated and yet so powerful.

They sank back on the bed together, legs entwined. Angie traced light, fleeting designs on his body, exploring him tentatively at first, and then with increasing daring and heat. She learned the long, unyielding lines of his legs, the lean strength of his slim, masculine hips, the rounded muscles of his arms, and the square planes of his broad chest. She learned that the back of his neck was highly sensitive to her tongue and that his buttocks tightened whenever she touched them.

And she learned that his power over her was awesome. He seemed to command her, deciding feverishly where to arouse her and then accomplishing it with the most delicate and sensual of touches.

When she had reached a plateau of desire that she was barely able to stand, she tugged at his shoulders and tried to bring his body over hers. "Please, Kyle," she whispered frantically. "Now."

He kissed her with a long, deep mastery that left her breathless. "Not yet, sweet," he answered. "We've only just started."

His mouth descended slowly and his tongue flicked at one taut nipple, bringing it to a rosy peak. He continued to tease her in slow, ragged circles, moving from one breast to the other and then slowly back again. Her breasts were round and firm, each sloping slightly to one side when she was lying down, and he lifted them gently in each hand to hold them within reach of his mouth. When she thought she would die from this caress alone, he slid down, kissing her body down its satiny length, lingering on the tender insides of her thighs and teasing the space in between.

Angie was no longer certain she was on the bed. They were floating several feet above it, free from earthly constraints.

She was almost weeping with need when Kyle slid his strong arms underneath her body, one beneath her shoulders and the other beneath her hips. He positioned himself carefully above her and then found the exact spot without reaching down to feel it. Before he entered her, he looked down into her open face, his blue eyes shining with desire and anticipation. Whereas before she had felt womanly and beautiful and warm, she now felt wanton and unfettered.

He was gentle with her at first, finding her center and letting her guide his descent inside. But as the new feelings overwhelmed them and her body adjusted unconsciously to his presence, they began to move with a timeless, erotic rhythm. Concentric rings of pleasure surrounded her like a halo, building and building to an unimaginable crescendo. She was barely aware that she was accompanying each thrust with an abandoned cry, and that her passionate sounds inflamed him even more.

Together they traveled through one rhythm and then another, until at last a pinnacle loomed before them. Angie lost all sense of time and place, all notion of one body joining with another. It no longer mattered where her body ended and Kyle's began, and she could no longer tell. Wild, vivid colors passed before her eyes as she toppled over, shaking and trembling helplessly in his arms.

Their descent from heaven was slow and languorous. Neither was in a hurry for the magic to end, but they knew they had to awaken and look at the new and beautiful unity they had created. At last Angie nudged gently and Kyle shifted his weight so that he was lying closely against her side. They opened their eyes.

"Hi," she whispered with a tiny smile.

He smiled back lazily, sated with her loving. "Hi."

A few long, comfortable moments passed as he traced the delicate line of her cheek.

"That was very clever of you," she murmured.

"Mmmm. What was?" His hand smoothed back wild tendrils of golden hair.

"The singing telegram."

He smiled again in acknowledgment.

"And the ticket."

The smile suspended. "What ticket?"

"To the exhibit. The one you sent with the messenger."

Kyle's hand dropped and the smile disappeared. The blue eyes opened wide and pinned her. "But I didn't send you a ticket. I thought you sent me one."

It was Angie's turn to be astonished. "No—I—" She stopped in confusion. "You mean we each thought... then who...?" Then it all came together. Of course! She fell back on the pillow, her head shaking back and forth in awed disbelief. "I should have known she would pull something like this." She let out a heavy sigh, still shaking her head.

"Samantha!" she and Kyle exclaimed simultaneously.

Chapter Seven

PROMPTLY AT NOON the next day, the contest between Supermom and Benny the Robot began, duly attended by a host of photographers, three New York network news teams, well-wishers on both sides, and, Angie noted wryly, Britt Shapiro Whittaker in all her glory.

Over three hundred women stood behind roped-off barriers across the street from the duo tract houses, cheering and shouting, while off to the side a faction from a newly formed group called Husbands' Liberation chanted a theme of their own.

> "Two, four, six, eight,
> Benny will eliminate!"

The women responded with rhythmic cries of

"Two, four, six, eight,
who do we appreciate?"

And in unison both men and women yelled the final line out together—"Angie! Angie! Angie!"—until the two sides created a discordant din that threatened to drown out the main proceedings.

But at last the two participants (not including Benny) faced off gamely in front of the cameras, playing their roles as adversaries so skillfully that no one suspected they had climbed out of bed—the same bed—only hours before.

"Supermom versus Benny the Robot," Britt Whittaker gushed to all the reporters. "The purpose of this contest is to determine just how replaceable the homemaker is."

Angie gave Britt a swift, hard look.

"Or irreplaceable," Britt amended, looking down at her notes as if something pertinent were written there. She continued her speech, explaining the rules to the reporters, but Angie didn't hear a word she was saying. It was impossible to feel the same way about the contest after last night with Kyle, and she didn't *want* to feel the same. He had surprised her completely, opening up parts of her that she had barely known existed. And the biggest surprise was that she had thought she was going to open *him* up, to reach into the layer of reserve that was camouflaged so effectively by his mercurial manner and gently discover a vulnerable, unique man who needed the special attention of a warm and caring woman. Instead, they had met each other halfway, a perfect blend of give and take that left both of them breathless at the intimacy that sprang up so naturally between them.

She looked longingly at Kyle, and he winked at her. His eyes were assessing the houses they were to compete in, and she followed his gaze curiously. Perhaps they could sneak over to each other's houses at night after the contest ended for the day. She was sure that was what he was thinking. It certainly wouldn't be hard to do.

The two houses in which they would live were complete mirror images of each other. Each house had the same square footage of front lawn, with the two garages right next to each other. The kitchens faced each other, and dual driveways in the middle led to the dark green garbage pails out in front. Large picture windows in front of each living room were curtainless, and Angie could easily see the comfortable furniture that had been placed inside. Even this aspect was exactly the same in both houses, right down to what appeared to be huge black stains in both armchairs in both living rooms.

"Well, they're true to their word," she said in an aside to Kyle, shaking her head. She pointed to the twin front doors, where dirty hands had left their mark. The whole scenario had an almost unreal quality. Everything was brand-new, letter-perfect, and preplanned. All up and down the street were spanking-new or almost-finished tract houses that looked just like the ones Angie and Kyle were to occupy, except that none of the houses had been sold yet. They would be the only people living on the block that week. It was a perfect setup. "Well," Angie continued, "it isn't exactly what I'd prefer, but you have to admit, it's very practical for this kind of a contest. I'm just not feeling in a very competitive mood... especially after last night." She looked up at him wistfully. "Are you?"

But he hadn't heard a word she'd said.

"Kyle?" Angie nudged him. He was so entranced with the rest of the neighborhood that he wasn't listening to her.

"Kyle, did you hear me?"

He began to chuckle under his breath, and Angie tried to frown him into propriety.

"What's so funny?" she hissed.

Waking up, he looked at her and pointed down the street at all the houses. "Looks like someone came by with a cookie cutter and baked up a model community overnight. I'd hate to come home drunk one night and try to figure out which house was mine."

"That will be easy," Angie said, and tossed her head toward the roofs of both houses. "Just look for the one with the black window."

Sure enough, two of the windows toward the back had been smeared with soot.

By now Britt was winding down her speech about homemakers and automation, and she began to introduce the two judges.

Bert and Ernie stepped up in unison beside her and stared somberly into the cameras. They were both dressed in black suits and each wore a stopwatch around his neck. The two clipboards they were holding told Angie that this was indeed a contest, and all at once she felt a sudden lurch in the pit of her stomach.

"Are you all right?" Kyle asked, observing her change in expression. He put his hand on her arm and discovered it was shaking a little. "Hey," he said lightly. "It's only a foolish little contest."

"Foolish?" Angie looked at the judges again and then at the two houses. "It wasn't so foolish to you when you first challenged me."

He gave her a warm, private smile. "That was before

last night." He looked around, and seeing that Britt was still rambling on, drawing all the attention to herself, he quietly took Angie by the hand and led her over to the side of the crowd.

"Someone will see us," she protested.

"Shhh." He let go of her hand and checked around furtively before continuing, "Let's make a pact."

"A what?"

"A pact, a deal."

"About what?"

"No competing," he said.

That took a second to sink in. "Isn't that dishonest?"

"Look, Angie. I don't want to give you a hard time."

"You won't." She smiled. "I can handle it."

Kyle sighed impatiently. "You still don't understand, do you, Angie? Look, let's agree to make the contest a draw, all right?"

She frowned, puzzled. "You're asking me to slow down? Deliberately?"

It was Kyle's turn to be puzzled. *"You* slow down?" He gave a short, deprecating laugh. "Uh, I thought *I* would slow *Benny* down, and—"

Angie gaped. "You're serious, aren't you?"

A flash of anger glinted in his eyes. "You want the truth?"

"Of course."

"Benny can work rings around you. You haven't got a prayer. Make up your mind, Angie. I'm offering you a way out. If you don't take it, don't blame me."

He opened his jacket and revealed a remote-control unit dangling from his belt. Angie inhaled sharply. She hadn't realized just how sophisticated Benny's backup system was.

"See this knob?" Kyle asked, pointing to a red dial

numbered one through ten. "It's Benny's gas pedal. The speedometer."

"Speedometer," Angie repeated, stunned.

"The higher, the faster." He looked at Angie and gave her a chilly smile. "What speed is yours set at?"

She didn't answer at all. She couldn't. This contest was not a joke, and it wasn't going to be a snap. Somehow she had managed to avoid realizing this before, and now she had no choice. She was in for the duration, and she would have to make the best of it.

"Angie?" Kyle's voice broke into her thoughts. "Are we agreed?"

"No," she said flatly, looking away. "Don't patronize me, Kyle. I don't need a handout. I accepted your challenge, and I intend to compete fairly. Besides, I wouldn't be so sure of myself if I were you. Speed isn't the only criterion, you know."

"Don't give me one of your lectures, Supermom," he said, holding up his hands as if to ward off an attack.

Britt sallied up to them, ready to begin. "Where's your daughter?" she asked Angie, peering through the crowd.

Angie didn't know Samantha's whereabouts herself. She suppressed a nervous flutter as she looked around hastily. Samantha was standing innocently next to Benny the Robot. She looked perfectly harmless, but with Samantha, Angie could never be sure.

"Come along," Britt summoned impatiently. "We're about to start."

While Britt rattled off the final list of rules, Benny sidled up silently behind her. To Angie's amazement, he proceeded to unwittingly steal everyone's attention by executing a peculiar but ingenious mechanical dance.

"Children are the untapped labor force in *any* household," Britt was expounding, but Benny zoomed around in front of her and let out a strange metallic noise.

"Down, boy," Britt tried to joke, patting Benny gingerly on the head. The little robot startled her by returning the gesture, but he went a step further. In front of everyone, he wrapped all six of his loving arms around Britt's slim, silk-clad form and exuded a low beeping noise that sounded vaguely like a cat with laryngitis.

"Uh, thank you, dear," she said, addressing Benny nervously. "You can let go now. Benny? Benny!"

By now, everyone was laughing.

"Oh, Mr. *Bennett?*"

Angie turned around and saw Kyle playing with the remote-control box. He put it back on his belt and met Angie's gaze calmly, as if challenging her to reveal his secret source of power—and to better it.

"Mr. Bennett!" Britt called helplessly.

Angie watched the trapped Britt in horrid fascination. At that moment, Britt was completely at Kyle's mercy.

"Benny! Disengage!" he commanded suddenly.

Benny retracted his arms at once, allowing Britt to escape. She promptly backed away, giving the robot a hostile glare.

"Well!" she huffed, patting her hair into place. Then she clearly remembered the cameras and flashed them a brilliant smile. "Uh—shall we begin?" she floundered. She turned to the two judges, who were waiting patiently and without expression for the contest to start. "Gentlemen, if you will take your positions inside the houses."

While the judges headed into the respective houses, Angie stole a hesitant glance at Kyle.

"Did you do that on purpose?" she demanded in a harsh whisper.

Kyle shook his head with exaggerated innocence. "He's

got a lot of preprograms that I don't control."

Angie looked down at the control box dangling from his belt beneath his jacket. She didn't believe him. And what was worse, he didn't seem to care. A stab of disappointment flashed through her as she thought about the blissful night they had spent in each other's arms. To her, it was a precious memory. But Kyle obviously had no regard for it at all. He was ready and willing to make a fool of her, and she would have to get through the next three days on her own. True, he had offered to make the contest a draw, but that was almost insulting. She wasn't so sure that Benny was going to win—fancy technology and all—and now she was more determined than ever to prove her superiority to a piece of machinery.

"Get on your marks!" Britt called out, and held up a starter's gun. "Part one of the contest is about to begin."

Angie looked at the greasy stain on the front door, and then down at Benny. Her decision was firm and clear. This contest was meant to be a fight to the finish, and that was exactly what she intended to make it—for better or worse.

"Last one in is a rotten egg!" she sang out.

A loud starter's gun exploded, and amid cheers and screams, Angie raced for the door.

"Let's go, Samantha!" she yelled.

She was halfway to the door when Benny zoomed by her on the adjacent walk at lightning speed and disappeared inside. It happened so fast that Angie had to stop and shake her head in disbelief. She wheeled around to see Kyle grinning at her. He had the controls in his hand, and his finger was on the red knob.

"Hope you're in shape!" he called after her.

Before she could reply, the door to the neighboring

Anything Goes   107

house opened and Benny reappeared with a bucket and a bottle of Mr. Clean. But when he tried to rub out the stain on the door with a sponge, nothing happened.

Angie gloated as Kyle hunched over Benny, the picture of perplexity. He examined the stain and rubbed it a few times with one finger, but his face registered a total blank.

"It has a strange cohesive factor," he mumbled.

"Cohesive factor?" Angie broke into loud laughter, and the competitive spirit rose up within her like a flag unfurling. "Brother, are you ever in for it!" She crossed her arms and watched the futile attempt, her confidence returning second by second. "It's going to take more than that red knob to beat me," she said saucily.

Kyle looked up wildly, as if expecting to find a solution in the air around him. "Come on, Samantha," Angie exulted, opening the door to the house. "Let's show our friend here a thing or two about the science of homemaking. By the time this day is over, there'll be nothing left of him but a bunch of burned-out transistors."

Within two hours, Angie had removed four major grease stains from a door, a chair, a lamp shade, and the kitchen ceiling. On top of that she managed to both clean the oven and defrost the refrigerator—and still coordinate cleaning the ceiling stain by soaking it on and off with a home solution of baking soda and Mr. Clean. The judges gave her an extra three merits for applying a new wax coating while removing the stain from the ceiling all at the same time.

"How's it going?"

Angie didn't hear Kyle's voice over the sound of the vacuum cleaner. While her left hand pushed the vacuum over the carpet, her right hand worked on removing a huge mound of melted-on candle wax from the dining room table.

"Samantha! Come in here at once!"

Kyle leaned against the door frame, amusing himself at the sight of Angie in action. He barely managed to get out of the way as Samantha bolted in on the double, a broom and dustpan in her hand. She hopped over to the table at her mother's direction.

"Does this look familiar, young lady?"

"My birthday party." Samantha beamed knowingly. "When Danny Shere blew out all the candles and they dripped onto the floor."

"Let's get going then. You know what I need, right?"

Samantha ran out of the room, and Kyle watched curiously as she returned a few seconds later with an iron and some paper napkins. After plugging in the iron, she handed it to her mother, who placed a paper napkin over the mound of dried wax.

Kyle's face lit up as Angie applied the iron over the napkin, and all at once the wax melted and was soaked up into the napkin. A few wipes of the table and it was totally cleaned.

"Oh, yes," Kyle said. "I remember that technique. You performed it at the shopping center demonstration a few weeks ago, right?"

Angie whirled around to see him grinning.

"Not fair!" she yelled, looking around for the judge. "Foul! Foul!"

"What do you mean, foul?"

"You can't come in here and steal my secrets. That's cheating."

Kyle held up a copy of the *Long Island Eagle*, which Angie immediately recognized.

"My column!" she protested.

"I read all of them—three times," he announced. "I had a heck of a time programming all this information into Benny's memory banks, but it was worth it."

"You *what?*"

He flourished the newspaper and grinned. "It's all on one little floppy disk inside Benny's stomach."

"Maybe he'll get indigestion," she muttered.

"Hey, now, why so sour?" Kyle looked wounded as he backed his way warily toward the door. "Sore losers make for bad sportsmanship."

"Oh?" She arched an eyebrow coldly. "Who says I'm losing?"

Kyle made it to the front door and pointed up and over. "He's already starting window cleaning."

"Impossible!" Angie cried, running over to have a better look. Sure enough, there was Benny, hanging by one claw out the upstairs bedroom window, his other five arms busily cleaning.

Angie immediately whipped into action.

"Samantha! Ammonia and water, at once. And don't forget the long-handled wiper."

She bounded up the stairs two at a time, Samantha right behind.

"So long, Supermom," Kyle said, laughing. "Or is it Batman and Robin?" He picked up the napkin that was hardened with the wax from the table and held it up. "What shall I do with this wax?" he called up after them.

Angie stopped at the top of the landing and looked back down. She was a little out of breath, but she managed a devilish grin and said, "Keep it, Kyle. As a souvenir of a valiant but futile effort. Yours, of course."

He gave her a mock salute and disappeared out the door.

"To the windows," Angie ordered. "You do the insides, I'll do the out."

Samantha immediately began in one bedroom while Angie headed into the other. It was a small, square room, furnished with a single bed, a dresser, and a nightstand, all brand-new. After opening the first window, she turned around and sat outside on the ledge. Down below, a few diligent photographers shot photos of her. Angie smiled cooperatively, posing for a few shots, when suddenly, out of the corner of her eye, she spied Benny speeding out the exact same window next door. The two adversaries squared off, ready to do battle, but Angie was no match for six arms. Within seconds, Benny had managed to clean the entire double set of windows.

"I don't believe it," she breathed as she hurried to get the first frame done. "That thing is definitely starting to irritate me."

Suddenly, without warning, she was hit by a heavy wet sponge.

"What the—" Another hit her square in the face, and water oozed down her back. When she looked across the way, Benny was preparing to throw a third one.

"Don't you dare!" She raised a fist at the robot, but all at once she realized who the real culprit was. Down below, she could see Kyle manipulating the remote controls with childish delight.

"What's the matter?" he called up tauntingly. "Can't take a little harmless prank?"

Angie opened her mouth to protest and then thought better of it. "I guess I can't. Can you?"

Before he could step out of the way, Angie had poured

her entire bucket of water on top of him. He was totally drenched.

"What's the matter, Kyle?" she echoed. "Can't you take a harmless little prank?"

Kyle made a strange sound that was a cross between a yelp and a growl when another, weirder humming sound began to emanate alarmingly from inside Benny. As Angie watched in fascination, the little robot ceased his frenetic movements and hung motionless by one claw out the window. He had been rendered totally immobile.

"Oh, no!" Kyle moaned. "Now look what you did." He held out his remote-control unit for her to see. "It's shorted out. Now I'll have to wait for it to dry."

"My heart bleeds for you." Angie laughed triumphantly. "Serves you right."

"I'm not beaten yet," he called up. He raced for the house, and a few minutes later appeared outside the same window from which Benny still dangled. Angie watched with growing trepidation as Kyle manipulated some buttons on Benny's stomach, and in a twinkling the robot had resumed cleaning the windows as if nothing had happened. Kyle threw her a triumphant smirk, and then sat outside on the flat ledge of the roof, casually surveying the street below. The careless smirk remained on his face as he leaned back with his hands folded behind his head.

"Benny's on total automatic pilot," he explained briefly. Then he removed the controls from his belt and carefully placed them on the roof to dry out. "Solid-state circuitry," he continued obligingly as he pointed at the wet control unit. "It'll be dry in an hour and then I'll be able to have him speeding rings around you. Which reminds me, I think he's ready to clean the bathtub."

Kyle leaned forward, careful not to lose his balance so high above the ground, and reached for the window. He missed a firm grip, but managed to move it slightly. With a loud bang, it suddenly shut tight.

Kyle tugged at it, but it was no use. He sat back to ponder his dilemma with as much dignity as he could muster. Angie watched this performance with a growing degree of enjoyment.

"He locked you out, didn't he?" she asked smugly.

"Benny!" Kyle called through the closed window. "Come here!"

There was no response.

"Benny!" Kyle raised his voice. "Come here!"

Angie started to whistle a meaningless tune as she finished up the first set of windows. Kyle was ominously silent the whole time, and Angie stole a glance at him. He looked so woebegone that she began to wonder if she should give him a break and let him in. No one else was allowed to help him, and it was dangerous for him to sit out there on the roof for so long.

Nawww, she decided. He looked so peaceful and harmless. After giving the windows a final rinsing and drying, she climbed back inside her house and went into the other room. The routine was the same except that the silence between the two adversaries seemed to increase weightily as she scrubbed away industriously and Kyle waited with murderous patience for his controls to dry out.

"How're you doing over there, Buck Rogers?" she said with a huge grin, and waved.

Kyle resolutely waved back and salvaged his predicament by basking deliberately in the afternoon sun while the photographers snapped his picture.

Anything Goes

Unfortunately for Benny, it took more than an hour for the controls to dry. During that time Angie managed to catch up and even move ahead of the robot, who was stuck in the bathroom cleaning the bathtub over and over like a science-fiction character in a time warp.

Angie was just taking out the garbage and waiting for the last huge load of laundry to dry when she stopped in the driveway to see how Kyle was doing. Sure enough, he was still lounging on the roof, furtively watching her progress.

"From what I understand," she called up to him, "you're going to have the cleanest bathroom in the Western world."

"I'll have no more ring around the rim," he answered tersely.

"Definitely not. I overheard Ernie the smiling judge say that Benny is practically sawing through the tub. I suggest taking a shower tonight." She continued her stroll down the driveway, but Kyle had been needled beyond the point of control. He jumped up, almost losing his balance, and tugged furiously at the window once more.

"Benny!" he shouted. "Come! Benny! Benny!"

Angie clutched the garbage she was holding and her heart skipped a beat as she watched his antics. It was enough that she was winning. Kyle was likely to fall off the roof at this rate. She remembered the sensual night they had shared and her heart melted. No matter what it meant to him, she couldn't dismiss it. She would show Kyle and everyone else what a good sport she could be.

After depositing the garbage, she ran next door and bounded up the stairs. Running down the hall, she caught a glimpse of Benny in the bathroom, doomed to cleaning the tub for all eternity unless someone intervened.

"Thataboy, Benny," Angie muttered. "You may not be smart, but you sure are persistent."

"Benny!" Kyle's muffled voice was still calling. It was all but drowned out by the constant drone of Benny's engines.

Angie headed into the bedroom and ran up to the window, where she found herself face to face with Kyle.

"Open up," he gestured. "Please?"

He looked like a soldier who had lost his regiment. Seeing him up close, Angie had to choke back a laugh. She opened the window and promptly climbed out to join him. The photographers immediately began snapping pictures of the two competitors perched together on the roof.

"What are you doing?" he asked wildly. Then he leaned inside and yelled, "Benny! Negate!"

They listened as the robot finally responded by trundling out of the bathroom.

"Unit seven, now!"

"I think he's heading down with the laundry," Angie said, patting Kyle on the arm. "No hard feelings, are there?"

Kyle shrugged uncomfortably. "I deserved that, I guess." He looked at her beseechingly, and she felt her firm resolve slipping. "I'll make it up to you tonight," he continued, his eyes brightening.

She touched his hand tentatively, remembering suddenly what his touch could do to her and not wanting the people below to see. "That's not necessary," she said slowly. "You've been chastened enough out here on the roof."

"I wasn't talking about that," he said, looking at her meaningfully. "Come on, Angie. Loosen up. Just because

Anything Goes   115

we're competitors doesn't mean we have to keep up our acts at night, when everyone else has gone home."

Angie was torn in two distinct directions. Yes, she wanted to share Kyle's bed—but not just for the duration of the contest. She wanted much, much more from him, but he seemed oblivious to the possibilities. "We'd better go back inside, Kyle," she said, avoiding his gaze.

She reached for the window and stumbled heavily, clutching the frame for support. The window closed abruptly as she leaned on it, and to her dismay, she found herself locked out on the roof with Kyle.

He laughed heartily and patted her hand amiably. "Welcome to the club," he said, settling back to wait. His laughter was infectious, and she decided that the best thing to do was join in.

"Friends again?" he queried, taking advantage of the new mood.

Angie thought fast as he held out his hand. She wanted desperately for Kyle to recognize and share her deeper concerns, but she was willing to go along with his playful overtures as well. "Friends," she agreed, shaking hands with him decidedly. Kyle beamed and kept her hand imprisoned in his as the photographers snapped away at the two opponents sitting on the roof holding hands.

"What about later?" he persisted, giving her hand an intimate squeeze.

"Maybe," she hedged, looking down.

She had no choice, really. There was no point in keeping him at arm's length. That would only belie her true feelings. But she realized all too well that her position with him was as precarious as their impromptu perch on the roof.

Chapter Eight

"Mom! Wake up. There's a skillion million people outside... Mom!"

The bedclothes over Angie's head remained a motionless shroud as Samantha shook them a few times for a sign of life. "Mom, come on," she urged. "They're about to start."

"Start?" A hand slowly crept out from beneath the sheets and groped around the nightstand for the clock. "What time is it, Samantha?" she croaked.

"Ten to seven."

"That late already?"

"I'll make breakfast," Samantha offered, skipping downstairs.

Angie had retracted her arm and was trying to drift back to sleep when she heard the sound of heavy footsteps entering the room, and another voice, more commanding than Samantha's, pierced her ears.

"Better get yourself moving, toots. There are several hundred reporters outside waiting to see you."

Angie grumbled without looking up. She could hear Britt opening her closet door, but she just wasn't ready to face it—not yet.

"Is this all you brought with you to wear?" Britt demanded. "You can't go in front of a half billion people dressed in worn jeans and a work shirt."

"There's always my Gypsy Rose Lee feathers as an alternative," Angie shot back. "Or how about my Lady Godiva outfit? You wouldn't know where I could get a horse this early in the morning, would you?"

Britt was not amused. "Look, Supermom," she said. "I know I'm not supposed to take sides in this contest, but frankly, it will be a blow to your dignity as a Supermom—not to mention your column—if you lose. So let's get moving."

"At the moment, it's not my dignity that I'm worried about," Angie groaned. "My arms feel like a ton of bricks. I must have lifted over a hundred pounds of laundry yesterday afternoon. And that creepy little pint-sized metal dwarf comes rolling out with the whole hundred-pound load in his arms as if he were carrying feathers."

"Yes, well, you have to admit, it *was* the highlight of the day," Britt remarked dryly. "He easily stole the limelight from you, as well as the front page of every newspaper in the Western world." She tossed down a bunch of what felt like newspapers, causing Angie to flinch violently.

Reaching out blindly again, Angie groped for the papers and grabbed the top one off the pile. Pulling it back under the covers, she managed to open her eyes and look it over.

"Well, isn't that just great. I spend a whole afternoon killing myself, and that blasted tin can gets all the publicity."

Sure enough, the front page was all but taken up with a picture of Benny balancing a hundred pounds of laundry in his many arms. Angie read the blurb aloud.

"'It does windows, too.'" She smirked. "Ha, ha. Does it say anything about the bathtub the little imp demolished?"

"Page three, column two," Britt acknowledged with a tinge of sympathy. "Right next to the cute little article about the two birds caught together in a love nest."

Angie turned the page and gasped. The gasp was followed by her bolting upright and tossing the covers off impetuously. She was now totally awake as she gazed at the picture of Kyle and her trapped on the roof together. The pictures had caught them holding hands, and the looks on their faces said it all. She hadn't realized how clearly her face had registered her true feelings. Her heart sank.

"Oh, great!" she moaned. "That's it. We're through. Now everyone will think the contest is a phony—and worse, they'll think I am, too." Blithely unconcerned with Britt's presence, she flipped through the other newspapers. The famous love nest picture appeared in every one.

"Terrific, that's all I need. Now I'll be known as Sell-out Angie or Two-faced Supermom, or worse, Super Sap."

"Never mind *that*," Britt said. "There's one thing that's even more important than your little tryst with Mr. Bennett."

Angie continued to flip through the newspapers until

her eyes suddenly focused on the blurb of a second-page article in the New York *Daily News*. There was no need for Britt to elaborate. The answer was staring her right in the face.

"Oh, my God," Angie breathed in horror. "I'm losing."

"I believe a more delicate phrase would be 'trailing somewhat.'"

"Not according to this article." She busily rummaged back over the other papers. Sure enough, they all had her way behind in every area. "That little mechanical spider is going to put me out of business. How did I ever let myself get into this mess?" Angie was all but lost in hopeless self-pity. She rubbed her eyes and then began woefully to rub her sore arms and legs.

"Well, it's not over," Britt reminded her. "You haven't lost *yet*. Now, I want you to get out there and show your stuff. Okay?"

But Angie was still aghast. "I'm ruined," she moaned. "Utterly ruined."

"You're merely *behind*, that's all," Britt said, trying to bolster her as best she could. "Now, eat a good breakfast and come out punching."

Samantha came bounding obligingly into the room, full of energy. "Breakfast is ready!"

She placed a tray of food on the bed and was about to leave when Angie stopped her in her tracks.

"Hold it right there, kiddo. I have a question I've been meaning to ask you. It's about those tickets you sent to Kyle and me."

Samantha looked back at her blankly. "What do you mean, Mom?" she asked, puzzled. "I didn't send any tickets. Maybe it was Britt?"

Angie transferred her gaze accusingly to Britt. "What

on *earth* are you talking about?" Britt asked irritably.

Angie explained, and although Britt continued to deny any involvement, her journalist's eyes gleamed at the scoop. She immediately tried to play the whole thing into an angle for her magazine.

"After your tryst yesterday afternoon, dear, it sounds *absolutely* intriguing," she cooed.

Half an hour later, they were standing in the spotless kitchen, where Ernie the judge was nosing around with his clipboard and Samantha was busy putting the dishes in the dishwasher.

"Might as well get started," Britt finally announced, heading for the door. "All set, everybody? Then let's get going. We've got a long day ahead of us."

"You all go first," Angie said. "I've got to prepare a little."

"Don't be *long*, dear," Britt warned as she and Samantha and the judge left the kitchen. Angie took a deep breath, counted to ten, and followed them a minute later. But she wasn't prepared for the roar of approval from the crowd outside, and she jumped back in before they could get a good look at her. "My God," she said to herself, leaning against the inside of the door. "They sound like hungry lions."

"Not as hungry as this lion." Before she could react, Kyle's arms were around her, making her jump and want to nestle against him at the same time. He smelled fresh and clean, and he kissed her quickly on the side of the neck.

"Where did you materialize from?" Angie whispered frantically.

"Ever hear of back doors?" he murmured huskily into her ear.

"Careful," she warned. "Ernie's in the next room." A

danger alarm went off in her head at their sudden contact, but she simply couldn't resist him. She did nothing to discourage his advances, and he reached out and took her in his arms.

"I don't care," he answered recklessly, his hands finding the curve of her waist and molding it possessively. "This morning they can do anything they want to me."

"Well," Angie said dubiously. "You're in a good mood. It wouldn't have anything to do with being miles ahead in this contest, would it?"

"Nope," Kyle answered. He kissed her teasingly on the forehead. "I just heard from my partner this morning. You remember, the inventor of the famous blob chair."

"Oh, yes—Alpha."

"Alpha the Great." He nodded. "My partner and cohort. He just had a big sales meeting last night, and it's looking good. Any time now, we could get a contract for Benny. And that," he added, pointing a finger at her, "is my ticket to success."

"That is what you wanted," she acknowledged slowly, but her face was anxious and drawn. "But where does it leave me?"

"Don't worry, Angie," he said earnestly. "Everything will turn out all right. You'll see." She wanted with all her heart and soul to believe that, but the contest was making it more and more difficult. Kyle kissed her again, and this time the contact was so long and deep that she was momentarily able to forget her troubles. Why was Kyle such a bundle of contradictions? He taunted her mercilessly, but she melted whenever he showed the slightest tenderness. When the kiss ended, he seemed to relax in a way she had never seen before. "I missed you last night," he confided, making her heart jump.

"I don't know why," she said innocently. "I seem to recall you making a little nocturnal visit to my room."

"Yes, but you fell asleep, remember?"

"I couldn't help it. I was exhausted." That was only partly true, of course. She had been too confused about her feelings for Kyle to know what to do.

"Well, at least you didn't have a headache," he said, undaunted.

Angie managed to change the subject. "After reading this morning's newspapers, I'd say we're both going to have one."

Kyle laughed carelessly and ran his hands through her hair.

"Don't you even care?" she protested, trying to squirm away.

"Hardly worth a second thought," he said as he drew her close again.

"But what about Benny?"

"Benny can take care of himself."

A loud, boisterous roar of laughter reached their ears from the crowd outside, and Angie turned anxiously.

"At this moment," Kyle explained, gesturing toward the door, "I've got him programmed to shake hands with everyone he comes in contact with. He'd make a great politician."

"You're winning, you know," Angie informed him ruefully.

"Oh?" His blue eyes caressed her face. "It must be my dynamite sexual technique."

"I was talking about the contest."

"It's not whether you win or lose," he murmured as he opened the top button of her dress, "but how you play the game." His hands started to reach inside her dress, but Angie stepped back.

"You're pretty confident, aren't you?" she asked resentfully.

Kyle looked down at her with an expression that was oddly vulnerable. "All's fair in love and war, Angie."

Love? War? She searched his face for a clue, but he was inscrutable, and Ernie's loud, decisive footsteps were coming closer and closer. Kyle immediately turned away.

"See you tonight," he whispered, kissing her softly before she could protest. He gave her a devilish smile, reminding her of a tomcat on the loose. "There's a bottle of Château Margaux in my fridge just waiting to be ravished."

Angie had the distinct feeling that he was talking about ravishing far more than the bottle of wine, but she said nothing. His remark about love and war had sparked her hopes, but with Kyle, she could never be sure. Maybe he was flippantly saying whatever popped into his head, feeling free to leave her with the consequences.

Angie wasn't taking any chances. Love is one thing, she decided. But now it's time for war. As soon as Kyle was out of the house, she mentally prepared to do battle. The moment she opened the front door, she was accosted from all sides by a huge roar of applause, whistles, and chants. Over eight different TV cameras were now set up high on top of trucks, and as she made her way into the sunlight, the constant clicking of camera shutters sounded like a flock of hungry birds snapping at her.

"Angie! Angie! Angie!" Thousands of people chanted in the streets and waved placards that showed their support for Angie and the American homemaker.

WE'RE NOT BEAT YET
ROUND TWO
ALL'S FAIR IN LOVE AND WAR

Kyle was just coming out of his house, and he, too, was overwhelmed by the crowd. Angie looked at him and then at a particular sign that caught their attention at once. It was a blown-up picture of the two of them sitting on the roof together holding hands. Underneath the caption read the words LOVE THY NEIGHBOR. Angie followed the sign down to its owner, who winked at her and smiled knowingly.

"Come on, you two," Britt called, waving them together. "Come on." She held their hands and spoke into a microphone as the reporters pressed closer.

"Are you still as confident as yesterday, Ms. Carpenter?" a reporter called out.

"I've just begun to fight!" Angie yelled into the microphone, and the crowd of mostly women shouted approval and applauded loudly.

Before the roar could die down, another question was shot at her. "What about those rumors of a romance?"

"Benny's not my type," she said, still holding on to her confident smile.

"How about Mr. Bennett?" another asked pointedly, to the delighted laughter of the crowd.

Kyle smiled as he waited for Angie to field that one.

"He's not Kyle's type either," she answered quickly, her eyes sparkling.

This was met by an energetic crescendo of applause and laughter that didn't stop for a full minute. Finally, Britt called for quiet.

"Today's events are as follows." She took out a list

and began reading. "Floor polishing, lawn care, general housework, food shopping, car troubles, and a full four-course gourmet dinner for ten."

"Uh—car troubles?" Angie asked. "That wasn't on the original list."

"Don't worry, dear," Britt assured her. "It's nothing you can't handle."

Angie looked involuntarily at Kyle's grinning face.

"Well," he said nonchalantly as the reporters moved back to give them room, "I think I'll just park myself on that chaise longue over there and watch the show begin."

And that's exactly what he did. "Benny's already pre-programmed for today's activities," he explained. "So if you don't mind..." He leaned back comfortably in the chair on the front lawn and picked up a newspaper, pretending to be oblivious to the clicking cameras that caught his jaunty pose. "Up, up, and away, Supermom," he said to Angie with a lazy grin.

"Samantha!" she called. Her daughter waited eagerly, like a dutiful soldier, for her new orders. "To the house!"

After a final wave at the cameras, Angie went about the task of beating Benny with renewed energy. Persistent cheering dominated the morning as the two adversaries went about their tasks. At first there was plenty of interest from everyone in the street, but the gradual realization that regular housecleaning was all that was going on soon discouraged all but the most stalwart. By late morning, the crowd had trickled from the original thousands down to a handful of devoted stragglers. Even the reporters packed it up, and the TV crews began milling around with Styrofoam cups of coffee, waiting for something exciting to happen. But not much occurred for quite a while.

Anything Goes

Meanwhile, Angie had managed to do all the floors just as quickly as Benny, and with Samantha's help, she actually found herself within sight of catching up a little. After all, Benny couldn't mow the lawn and be in the house waxing all at the same time. It wasn't until Angie found herself walking alongside Benny to dispose of some filled plastic garbage bags that things began to go haywire.

Each of them was carrying two bags. Benny held one in each claw, while Angie lugged hers as best as she could. She finally had to put both down and carry them one at a time while Benny easily made it down to the cans in one trip.

"You think you're pretty clever, don't you, Benny?" she asked.

The robot didn't even beep as he easily removed the lid from one of the pails. But as it prepared to drop the first bag in, Angie was suddenly struck by a delightfully devious idea.

"Okay, you little creep," she said. "Let's just see how smart you are." And with that, she gently nudged Benny's garbage pail a full foot over to the left. Sure enough, the little robot dropped the bag with mechanical precision onto the street. The bag promptly burst open, spewing garbage all over the ground.

"Just as I suspected," Angie said calmly, and turned toward the photographers, who were gathering in droves for a shot. "He's only programmed to drop garbage at that one exact spot," she explained. "Like a blind person who memorizes where everything is, Benny has to rely on the information he's been given in advance."

She walked back triumphantly, and after depositing her second bag of garbage, gave Kyle a deliberately challenging glance. Before Benny could clean up his garbage, Samantha and Angie had already completed mowing the lawn.

But Kyle caught up quickly. He immediately sent Benny into action. Naturally, the robot mowed his lawn in less than half the time it had taken her. By the time she hooked up the water sprinkler, Benny was already trimming the hedges.

"I'll never win," Angie moaned, and plunked herself down on the grass to ponder her dilemma. The sprinkler was still waiting to be turned on, but she was rapidly losing her will to go on. Kyle was right, she mused morosely. That little robot *could* put the American housewife out of business. Not to mention a certain Supermom with a helpful hints column. She glanced resentfully over at Kyle, who was smugly operating his blasted controls, and he gave her a friendly smile.

"What's the matter?" he teased. "Has Supermom the Invincible fallen down on the job?" He expertly directed Benny to shave the hedges on the far side of the house, and Angie quickly placed her sprinkler at the very edge of her lawn, only a few short feet from where Kyle was lounging.

"This ought to cool you off," she said as she turned the switch. The water immediately leaped into action, spraying a long stream onto Kyle's grass and onto Kyle himself, who jumped up in time to save his remote-control unit from yet another douse. Once out of danger, he examined the unit carefully with a confident smile.

"Nice try, Angie. But rather juvenile, don't you think?"

Angie ignored him and turned to readjust the hose. Suddenly, a hard tug sent her sprawling onto the wet grass. "Oh!" she exclaimed and looked up to see three pairs of claws pulling at her hose, attempting to drag it away. "Samantha!" she ordered. "Quick! Grab hold and pull!"

"Oh, boy, a tug of war!" Samantha yelled gleefully.

Angie looked up in horror. Kyle had turned on his sprinkler so that Angie's hose was positioned directly in the path of his spray. If she lost the tug of war, she'd get a dose of her own medicine. And if she let Benny carry off her hose, she wouldn't be able to water her lawn.

The camera crews and photographers got their gear in order and began filming the tussle.

"Oh, no," she cried, feeling the hose slipping, "we're losing! Pull, Samantha!"

But try as they might, they were no match for Benny. He easily towed them into the line of fire, and in a matter of minutes Angie and her daughter were drenched.

Kyle was laughing on the sidelines. "That was quite a show!" He applauded loudly. Finally, he let Benny give up the hose, and Angie angrily pressed the water from her hair as he gave her a casual wave. "See you around," he called. "Come on, Benny. Let's drive into town for our shopping spree."

Just then, Bert and Ernie appeared from the opposite houses, and in uncanny unison, as if programmed exactly like Benny, they walked over to the two new cars parked in the two driveways.

"I'll be right with you," Angie called to Bert. "I'm just going to get out of these wet clothes. Samantha! Get ready to go shopping for food." She paused to turn on her sprinkler, but stopped dead when she saw what Bert and Ernie were doing. With absolute precision, they each approached the right front tires of the two cars and proceeded to let out all of the air. Angie's heart sank. Quick, she thought. A jack. A wrench. Good grief, what next?

Kyle had a very different reaction. He sat up casually and worked the controls on his belt, as if this latest snag were only a minor annoyance. Angie watched in dismay as Benny came whizzing out of the house. He wheeled around to the trunk of the car, extracted the necessary tools and the spare tire, and spun over to the flat tire in a total of fifteen seconds. With one arm, he actually raised the car, with a second arm he was detaching the flat tire, and a third arm was already lifting the new tire into place.

Samantha crept up behind her mother and watched this performance in silent awe. "Geez," she said finally. "We'll never make it."

"I know," Angie answered miserably. She stood up and sighed. "Go and get the jack, Samantha. Let's get this over with."

Samantha ran off and Angie trudged over to her car just as Benny was finishing up. When he was done, Kyle got up, brushed himself off, and came sauntering over. "See you later, Supermom," he called, climbing into the driver's seat with Benny seated next to him.

"Later," Angie repeated glumly, collapsing onto the grass and watching them drive off. "If I'm still alive."

Chapter Nine

"I'M THE BARBER of Seviiiille!!" Kyle's singing was enthusiastic but utterly off key. "I'm the Barber of Seviiiille! Figaro-o-o! Figaro, Figaro, Figaro!"

Disgruntled, Angie sat in the lawn chair outside, her arms folded primly in general dissatisfaction as she watched Kyle turn his hamburger on the grill in the backyard next door. He was wearing an apron with the words *Kiss the cook* written on the front, and sported a huge chef's hat and a heavy, padded glove. Standing dutifully next to him, holding a tray of coleslaw, potato salad, and extra meat patties, was Benny.

"I'm the barber of Seviiiille!! I'm the barber of Seviiiille!!"

"You'll never make the Met!" Angie called out when she couldn't take any more.

He gave her a quick glance and smiled serenely as

the flames rose up into the evening sky. "Figaro-o-o! Figaro! Figaro!"

"Hey, Caruso!" Angie called over. "Put a lid on it, would you, please? I'm trying to rest my ears."

Kyle raised his cooking fork high into the air and held the last note an extra-long time until his breath gave out. "FIGAROOHHHHHHHHHH..."

Samantha walked over to the fence and applauded loudly.

"Bravissimo," she called enthusiastically. "Bravissimo!"

Kyle bowed to her gallantly with a graceful sweep.

"It means extremely neat," Samantha explained earnestly.

"I know. Thank you, thank you, thank you," he said merrily. "Now, for my next number—"

"Nooooo, no more!" Angie protested. "Stop! Desist! Enough!"

"What's the matter, Carpenter?" he called out. "Can't stand the heat?"

"Just the singing, Bennett."

He took a good look at her dejected pose and put down the cooking fork. Leaving Benny to guard the fort, he marched over to her yard, saluting a receptive Samantha, who tagged along behind him.

"Hmmmmm," he said, stroking his chin in the manner of a seasoned psychiatrist. "I think I see the problem."

Angie ignored the condescension and scowled. "Oh you do, do you?"

"Yes, it is quite obvious. You suffer from an acute case of the blues—to put it in scientific terms." He looked analytically at Samantha, who was just barely restraining her giggles. "Aha," he nodded sagely, poking at Samantha's side. "I see *you* suffer from acute laughter!"

Samantha burst out laughing. "Yes!" she screamed helplessly as he began a full-scale attack on her ribs. "Oh, please! Kyle! No more!"

"No more?" He gave Samantha a puzzled glare and poked her once more. "And why not?"

Samantha fell onto the grass as he continued to tickle her. She was rolling all over the grass and Kyle was doggedly pursuing her when suddenly he stopped and looked at Angie.

"Hold it a second," he said as he apparently realized something. Looking down at Samantha, who was now trying to protect herself with her hands, he grinned wickedly and transferred his gaze to Angie. Then he swiveled back to Samantha, who was still giggling between gasps.

"You are not the patient here," he said, as if deducing a brilliant point. "You do not need the famous tickle cure." He focused on Angie, still sitting sourly in the lawn chair, and grinned again.

"Please, God, spare me," she muttered.

"Don't worry about a thing, *madame*. I will cure you of this dreadful malady." He raised his hands and advanced toward her ribs, ready to launch an attack.

"I'm warning you, Bennett."

"It won't hurt a bit," he promised, and was almost upon her when she jumped up and stood on the opposite side of the chair, her face a mask of warning.

"Forget it, Kyle. I mean it."

"I am deeply wounded," he said with mock stiffness, letting his hands fall in defeat. "I may never practice medicine again."

"Promise?" Angie asked ardently. She sat down heavily in the same position as Kyle dropped his stance and eyed her seriously.

"Know what's wrong with your mother, Samantha? She's lost her sense of humor."

"That's not all I've lost," Angie said bitterly. "Try my reputation, my job, and my self-respect for starters—not to mention this ridiculous contest. After today's performance, my name will be mud from coast to coast. By tomorrow, the papers should totally annihilate me from the face of the earth. I'm dead, finished, obliterated. But other than that, I'm just fine."

"In that case," Kyle quipped, "would you like your last meal served à la Bennett?"

Angie looked surprised, but nodded weakly. "If that's an offer to cook for me, you're on."

Kyle headed back to the grill and threw on two more beef patties. "Dinner in a chaise longue, coming right up," he announced.

"Do you think you could manage to serve it without that triumphant smirk on your face?" Angie asked.

"Sorry, but the smirk comes with the service." He waved Samantha over and handed her a paper plate. "If you will just hold this plate, *mademoiselle*, I will fill it with one scrumptious hamburger bun." He flipped the bun up in the air and it landed squarely in the middle of the plate.

"How dexterous," Samantha said.

"You ain't seen nothin' yet."

Angie watched Kyle charm her daughter, not wanting to admit that he easily charmed her as well. He was so carefree and independent, so different from her own boxed-in propriety. He continued his performance, deftly flipping the hamburger up and over his shoulder. Before her startled eyes, he did a complete turn holding the roll in back of him and caught the burger between the two slices.

"I'm impressed, Bennett," Angie called grudgingly. "You missed your calling. You should have been a clown."

Kyle merely smiled, tipping his hat and preparing another hamburger for himself. He brought the food over and they ate in neutral but companionable silence.

"So what do you say to a little stroll with me tonight?" he asked Angie amiably as they all finished up the burgers. "I've got a large bottle of wine I've been keeping chilled since this morning, and I thought maybe you and I could take a long walk in this ridiculously empty neighborhood and call a temporary truce."

Angie hesitated. There could be no harm in a walk, could there? Besides, she knew she would do anything at this point to maintain her tenuous relationship with Kyle Bennett. She looked pointedly at Samantha, who threw her hands up. "I know, I know," Samantha said. "You want me to hurry up and finish eating so I can go inside and see if there's something for me to do, right?"

"No," Angie corrected. "I'd appreciate it if you'd eat slowly. Then I'd like you to go inside and take a bath and get ready for bed."

Samantha immediately wolfed down the rest of her food. "I'm bored!" she announced dramatically. "There's no one to play with around here. There's no TV. I have to go to bed before the fireflies come out. And now I can't even play in my own backyard. It's just so odious, Mom." She turned a pleading gaze on Angie. "Can't I just stay up until it gets dark out? On account of you can't see fireflies until it's dark?"

Angie was sympathetic but reluctant. "Sorry, honey, but we have a big day tomorrow. I'm going to need you more than ever."

Sulking, Samantha stood up and began to walk away, kicking the ground in front of her.

"Hey, wait a second," Kyle said. Samantha paused hopefully. "How would you like to play with Benny?" To Samantha's glee, Kyle removed the control box from his belt and handed it to her.

"Are you sure?" Angie asked archly. "After all, he's your star player. Do you really want to give away your trade secrets?"

"Don't worry about it," Kyle answered. "There's a lot more to Benny than you know. I don't mind if Samantha wants to fiddle around with him a little, as long as she's careful. You will be careful, honey, won't you?" Samantha nodded vigorously. "Good. Now, this turns him on," he pointed out, "and this makes all the arms move." He went through each of the controls until Samantha had the whole routine down. "Just don't throw this red switch, whatever you do," he warned. "Okay?"

Samantha nodded again and reviewed the controls once more before taking a first try. She hesitated a second, but Kyle encouraged her.

"Go ahead," he said. "Bring him over here."

Samantha switched the controls cautiously and, after pushing a lever, waited tensely in anticipation. Within moments, the little robot rolled along the grass and came to a full stop in front of them.

"Would you like to take him for a walk?"

"Oh, boy!" She nodded eagerly, and a few minutes later robot and girl were parading out of the backyard.

"Just for fifteen minutes, Samantha!" Angie called. "Then it's bath- and bedtime."

The minute they were gone, Kyle rolled over next to Angie's chair and reached for her hand.

"What happens if she throws the red switch?" Angie asked curiously. "It's not dangerous, is it?"

"No," Kyle assured her, "just complicated. It adds auto pilot to the controls, aside from voice command and manual. If you don't know what you're doing, you can drive Benny crazy."

"Not as crazy as he's driven me," Angie said ruefully. "After Benny's performance today, I'm ready to concede."

"Don't be silly," Kyle said. "Where's your fighting spirit?" He sat up and brought her hand toward his mouth, kissing it gently. Angie melted.

"Kyle," she confided, too upset to think about maintaining her composure, "your little invention ran rings around me today in that supermarket. I never saw anything like it. He *is* a homemaker's dream. I admit it fully. No contest. You win."

"Just because he can shop faster?"

"*Faster!*" Angie was stunned. "*Faster?* Try at the speed of light. I would never have believed it. You'd think Benny had eyes in back of his head the way he can take six different cans of soup down from the shelf all at the same time."

"He *does* have eyes in back of his head," Kyle explained. "It's simple radar mixed in with his ability to read computer printouts on the labels. Of course, I help him along at times."

"And what about putting away all those groceries?" she persisted, her dismay mounting. "It took me a good forty-five minutes." She shook her head in defeat and laughed grimly. "Samantha and I carried two bundles inside the house while Benny carried six. We took forever to put all the groceries away while Benny did it in five minutes. We took an hour to wax a floor, and Benny did it in one third the time. Hell." Angie shrugged. "I may as well pack up and go home now. You've as good as won."

Kyle looked at her sternly. "I'm surprised at you, Supermom. Where's your determination? The contest isn't over yet."

"Well, I wish it were," she moaned. "Put me out of my misery."

There was a long pause. "Are you willing to talk about a draw now?" he asked.

"Oh, Kyle." Angie's eyes filled with tears. "No, no, it's too late for that. If you win, it will be fair and square. Besides, if we faked it now, everyone would know it—especially after today." She sat up and blinked back the tears, ordering herself to be a good sport. "Now, how about we partake of that bottle of wine?" she suggested, forcing a cheerful tone.

"And then partake of each other afterward," he suggested.

He leaned over to kiss her just as Benny and Samantha returned from their excursion.

"Ohh, excuse me." Samantha giggled knowingly.

Angie adjusted herself and cleared her throat. "Ready for bed, honey?"

"I guess," Samantha said.

"Say," Kyle suddenly suggested. "How would you like Benny to sit for you tonight while your mother and I go out for a walk?"

"Awwright!!" Samantha hooted.

"Is that safe?" Angie asked, concerned.

"I'll just put Benny on automatic guard. He'll do fine.

Besides, we won't go far." He looked out front into the street and shrugged. "We can stick around the neighborhood and keep an eye on the house the whole time."

"Well, I don't know," Angie said thoughtfully.

"Aww, Mom. Come on. It'll be fun," Samantha pleaded, and turned to Kyle. "Can Benny play checkers?"

Kyle reached over and pressed a series of buttons on Benny's breastplate. "He can now."

"I want you in bed by eight-thirty and no later," Angie relented.

"Oh, boy! Come on, Benny!" Samantha wheeled around and headed inside with Benny bringing up the rear.

"Don't worry," Kyle said reassuringly. He replaced the remote-control unit on his belt and patted it. "You'll be able to hear everything that's going on in the house." As Kyle flipped a switch, Angie was surprised to hear Samantha's voice from the control box coming through as on a walkie-talkie.

"Now, here's the checkerboard and checkers," Samantha's voice crackled over the air. "You can be black and I'll be the red. I go first."

"We can hear her just fine," Kyle said.

"Just so long as she can't hear us," Angie added, eyeing the bottle of wine.

After opening the wine, Kyle grabbed two paper cups, and together he and Angie walked silently in the warm night air. Row after row of empty cookie-cutter houses stretched as far as the eye could see, and they made their way along the pristine, winding streets and newly paved roads. The longer they walked, the more they drank, but Angie managed to keep a steady ear tuned to the control box as she listened to her daughter's voice. By the time they got to the end of the development, Angie's head was spinning from too much wine and her feet were growing more and more unsteady.

"Whoops!" she stumbled, and Kyle caught her in time to save her from a bad fall.

"Careful, there," he warned, swaying a little.

"Careful yourself," Angie admonished. "You're as tipsy as I am."

He lifted the wine bottle up to his eyes and examined the contents. "I'd say we drank more than half the bottle."

"Are we getting drunk?" Angie asked. She hadn't been drunk since her divorce.

"Naww," Kyle said after a moment's thought. "Not yet, anyway. But we will be." He poured more wine into both their cups and raised his glass in a toast. "To all the homemakers who will fill all these empty houses," he said, gesturing in a wide arc. "May you all manage to find—" He stopped and looked around for a second, laughing at some silly thought. "May you all manage to find your house in the dark," he concluded, and clinked his cup against Angie's.

"An appropriate toast," she agreed, and drained her cup dry.

Kyle splashed more wine into their cups, and again made another toast. "To us," he said groggily. "But especially to you. You really are a Supermom, Angie. I didn't realize it before."

"What?" She didn't hide her surprise.

"I saw what you did to your house," he explained hesitantly. "I wouldn't have thought of those things."

"Like what?"

"The little touches. Like fresh flowers. The pictures you hung on the walls. The afghan thrown over the couch.

And the plants hanging in the windows." He spoke with so much admiration that Angie had to smile.

"Those were no big deal," she answered honestly. "I just couldn't stand the sterility—I had to do something. You could easily duplicate all those things tomorrow."

"Easy for you," Kyle corrected quietly. "There's more to this business of being a homemaker than I realized. I never noticed those things were missing until I saw you had added them. You have a special touch, Angie. You have the ability to take any place, even a manufactured environment like this, and make it into a real home." He took her hands in his and looked down at her earnestly.

Angie's hopes leaped along with her pulse. She couldn't believe Kyle was talking to her like this after the rigors of the contest. She could see that he wasn't just saying all this to make her feel better. He really meant it, and he looked almost humble in his sincerity.

"Ah, so you do appreciate me, Kyle," she said tremulously, her eyes glimmering.

"Of course I do!" he cried, looking startled. "You're like a flower that keeps opening and opening, constantly surprising me with new and wonderful forms of beauty."

Suddenly, Angie was floating a foot above the ground, heady with his praise. He had no idea of his power over her. She fell completely under his spell when he wanted her there, but she was fired with the knowledge that he seemed to be drawing closer and closer to her. And he had been like a magician with Samantha. The sassy little girl had nestled under his wing with unerring instincts. Kyle had effortlessly forged a place for himself in their lives. A pang went through Angie as she thought about the effect on her daughter if Kyle should just as abruptly take his leave. Then she remembered her daughter alone in the empty house. "Samantha!" she exclaimed. "I hope she's all right."

"Shhh," Kyle put up a finger and smiled. "Listen."

They put their ears to Kyle's control box and listened carefully. Sounds of water running were followed by gurgling sounds.

"Brushing her teeth," Angie deduced.

The water was turned off and a light switch clicked off as well.

"I hope she heads up to bed now."

Sure enough, footsteps and Benny's humming came across loud and clear. They were followed by a heavy thumping, and Angie looked up at Kyle, puzzled.

"They're going up the stairs," Kyle realized.

A door squeaked open, and then sheets were pulled down as the bed creaked from the weight of Samantha jumping in.

"God, I feel as if I'm spying on my own daughter," Angie mumbled.

"Good night, Benny," she heard Samantha say. There was a loud, wet noise as Samantha kissed Benny good night.

Angie looked at Kyle and smiled, no longer worried, when suddenly Samantha added, "Oh, and good night, Kyle and Mom. I know you're listening."

Angie stopped dead in total surprise, and Kyle overcame his astonishment with a laugh. "I never told her," he mused. "She must have guessed."

"That daughter of mine never fails to surprise me."

They laughed gently together, and Kyle clicked his cup against hers. "To Samantha," he said. "May she never fail to surprise us."

"Oh, she won't," Angie assured him. "Let's just hope

her vocabulary doesn't get to the point where we can't understand her."

"As long as *we* understand each other," Kyle said, looking into the depths of her eyes. He put his arm around her and brought her close to him. "To us," he said gently. "May we always communicate." He kissed her quietly, but the kiss grew swiftly into a long, ardent exchange that was augmented by their growing state of dreaminess. "Mmmm," Angie murmured contentedly against his lips. "You are delicious." They were standing in front of a perfect, empty house with an immaculate lawn, and they were completely, blissfully alone. She could feel his heart pounding through his shirt, and the realization that her mere touch could excite him so ignited her own senses.

"Come," he whispered urgently, taking her hand and leading her onto the lawn.

Angie hesitated. "Here? What if someone sees us?"

"In this neighborhood?" Kyle looked around and laughed raggedly. "Don't be ridiculous. Who would come around here?"

"Just the same," Angie said. "I think I'd feel better if we were inside."

With a reluctant nod of agreement, Kyle turned back dizzily and clasped her hand. "Oh, boy, that wine was stronger than I thought," he said.

They steadied each other awkwardly and then began to walk, Angie going in one direction and Kyle in the other. "This way," they said in unison as they pointed in opposite directions.

Angie swayed around for a dizzying 360-degree panoramic view of the entire development. "What street were we on?" she asked suddenly.

"No street signs around here," Kyle replied. "They haven't put them up yet."

"Well, I think they should name a street after you," Angie announced. "Kyle Drive."

"Right at the intersection of Carpenter and Benny, right?"

"Right." Angie swayed once more and they collapsed against each other. When she looked up, her eyes were somehow spinning all the houses around, mixing them into a blur. "All the same," she said with a giggle.

"And all deserted. Kind of spooky, isn't it?"

"Definitely Twilight Zone."

They drank the rest of the wine and Kyle studiously examined the bottle's contents. It was empty.

"No more," he announced groggily.

"No more," Angie echoed.

Kyle stroked his chin and laughed at their predicament. "The proverbial drunks trying to find their house late at night in the model development community," he quipped.

"So, now what do we do?" Angie looked around one more time and pointed at each identical house. "Cookie-cutter houses all in a row. Which one is mine? Eeny-meeny-miny-mo."

Kyle perused the area impatiently, as if hoping to spot a landmark, but none existed. He gave up, put his arms around her, and gave her another long, timeless kiss. "All I know is that by hook or by crook, I'm going to find out where we live, and then I'm going to find a bed."

A good fifteen minutes later, they found themselves more lost than before. The houses all seemed to be mirror images, and Angie, who was more tipsy than she knew, was also feeling pleasantly and undeniably aroused.

"I want you, Angie," Kyle said huskily as he held her in frustration.

"First find the house," she wailed.

"The incentive is great, but the task is impossible." Kyle shook his head. "What I may need is a cold shower. It will sober me up and dampen my frustration at the same time."

"What we need is a homing pigeon," Angie replied.

No sooner had she said that than Kyle began to think. The thinking turned into a huge grin, and all at once Kyle was laughing at himself. "That's it!" he exclaimed. "A homing pigeon." He pulled the control unit from his belt and held it up. "And here it is."

Turning up the volume, he held the speaker to Angie's ear. All she heard was a steady rhythm of wind.

"What's that wind sound?" she asked.

"Samantha sleeping. We'll just follow it home. The louder it gets, the closer we are." He grabbed her hand and together they marched in the direction of the house. As it turned out, they were only a half-block away.

"Well, that wasn't so difficult," Kyle said, relieved. "Your place or mine?" he asked with a straight face.

Angie didn't hesitate. She wanted him searingly, and nothing was going to stop her from letting the passion between them blossom once more. "Yours," she decided quickly. "I don't want to wake Samantha. And I certainly don't want Benny marching in on us."

Kyle lifted her in his arms and carried her right into the house. Out of breath and panting, they held hands and ran lightly up the stairs, darting into Kyle's room.

"I think the ceiling is spinning around," Angie remarked.

"Oh, Angie." He gathered her close and kissed her. "You're adorable when you're crocked."

"So are you," she answered gravely. "So are you."

Their kisses were slow and dreamy, sweeping them back into that special world they had created only for them. Angie fell back and let out a long, rapturous sigh as Kyle watched her. It was so very good to be with him again. How could she have ever doubted the immediacy of this? She needed it with a yearning she had never known.

"Lovely," he murmured. "You are so lovely."

All the tensions and anxieties of the day were drained out of her as he coaxed and soothed her tired body. Lovingly, he undressed her, letting her clothes slip to the floor with a whisper, his eyes raking her bare flesh as each item fell away. Angie was tired and nervous and giddy from wine, and she needed desperately to find solace in Kyle's arms. She groaned with pleasure as he teased each breast and brought it to fullness, and her legs opened shamelessly to encourage him as his hand slipped over her torso in pursuit of her femininity.

"Please, Kyle," she pleaded, sudden tears stinging her eyes. All at once she realized how much had happened, and how much he meant to her. It wasn't just the contest, and it wasn't just that she was worried about its outcome. In this quiet, unreal setting, lying naked and vulnerable in the power of his caresses, she knew that it was much too late to negotiate anything. She had lost her heart to this mercurial, unreadable man, and she wanted nothing at this moment except his love.

"Shhh," he whispered soothingly, his hand grazing the insides of her thighs. "I'm here, Angie. And I won't leave until you are filled and overflowing."

Angie sighed tremulously and vowed to take what she could. He was talking only about physical satisfaction, but she wanted so much more. She gasped and lost all sense of reality when his probing hand found her womanly interior. The light butterfly strokes brought her quickly to the brink of fulfillment, and she shuddered deliciously beneath him.

"God, Angie," he cried, watching her unbridled passion, "you are exquisite. I have to have all of you, to know everything there is." His head bent to taste each ripened breast, and descended to leave moist circles on her soft stomach. When his hands moved down to open her thighs, she almost cried out with anticipation.

In a moment, his tongue was teasing and exploring her warmth, sending bolts of lightning through her blood. Angie's mind and soul focused on a single point of pleasure, and she pursued it and craved it until it overcame her. Her entire body trembled violently and her back arched as she crashed over the edge.

"Kyle..." she whispered brokenly. "Oh, Kyle..." She sat up dizzily, wanting suddenly to give him as much pleasure as he had given her. She pushed him down gently, and straddled him, relishing the look of hungry anticipation that flamed across his face.

Whereas before Angie had been a lush receptacle, drinking in and savoring sensation, she was now a willing server, pouring out her gratitude and love. She caressed and kissed and tantalized, starting at his powerful shoulders, moving down to his taut, male nipples, and continuing around his hard, flat belly. His long, lean legs were her next targets, and at last she concentrated solely on the masculine source of his desire.

Kyle seemed to spin into another world as she touched

it, and she was inspired to lavish every ounce of skill on her caresses to give him as much pleasure as he had given her. When he could bear no more, he gathered her into his powerful arms and covered her body with his.

They joined together quickly, feverishly, letting the overwhelming passion drive them with its own force. As they spiraled together, Angie's eyes misted with tears. Never would she forget the magnificence of this union.

As they approached the timeless place that took them over the edge and beyond, she wanted desperately to cry out her love and her need for him.

But even in the highest planes of her passion, she didn't dare.

Chapter Ten

"ANYTHING GOES," BRITT announced the next morning to the huge crowd of reporters and fans. She put an arm around both Kyle and Angie and she crunched them closer together. Angie mustered a brave smile and waited. She had dragged herself out of Kyle's arms at dawn to stagger back to her own bed, and her exhaustion was offset by her curiosity. "In just a few minutes," Britt continued, "our two contestants will each be allowed inside the other's house."

"To do what?" Angie asked cautiously. "Clean it?"

"Oh, no." Britt laughed. "Quite the opposite. You will have just fifteen minutes in which to do as much damage as possible," she finished brightly.

Kyle and Angie exchanged startled glances.

"Uh—within reason, right?" Angie asked carefully.

"Not at all," Britt answered, effectively squashing

Angie's last hope. "This is a no-holds-barred contest." She gave Angie a saccharine smile. "Remember today's theme, dear—anything goes."

A flush of excitement rippled through the crowd as everyone realized the full impact of this announcement.

"The life of every homemaker is fraught with challenge," Britt went on dramatically. "Tonight is the night you've invited ten people for a lovely formal dinner, but *just* when you think you'll have a quiet, busy day of cooking, disaster strikes."

"So this is going to test our ability to cope in an emergency, is that it?" Kyle asked.

"That's right. Dinner at six," Britt concluded cheerily. She winked at a camera. "And your guests will be on time." Holding up a stopwatch, she said, "Contestants on your marks... you've got fifteen minutes to do your best—or should I say your worst... go!"

The crowd burst into cheers, but they subsided quickly when neither contestant moved. Angie was about to dash into the house when Kyle suddenly burst into laughter.

"What's so funny?" She scowled.

He shook his head and, to the chagrin of the entire audience, marched into his own house. Angie was just as perplexed, and without a thought to the clock running, curiously followed right behind. He was still laughing when he turned around, but he stopped when he saw the look on her face.

"Fourteen minutes!" Britt called into the house.

"You'd better get started, Kyle," Angie said, but still he didn't move.

His blue eyes met hers with a candor that made her want to cry. She loved those eyes, and she loved the face that held them.

"Look, Angie," he said quietly. "This contest is getting out of hand. What do you say we call a truce for this last day? I won't do too much damage to your house if you won't destroy mine." Angie was silent. "What do you say?"

She looked up at him and saw the same flawless confidence, the same aura of power she had felt that day in her kitchen when he had been so sure of convincing her to compete. It still rankled her, but she didn't have a prayer unless she agreed. And if only she could believe that he was making his offer because he cared about her, not because he was growing tired of the contest. But he had never said any such thing, and she wasn't about to make a fool of herself over intentions that weren't really there.

"Come on, Angie," he wheedled softly. "I'll go easy on you. I promise. I know you need a break."

"Not from you," she maintained stubbornly. "I don't want any pity."

"Look, you admitted yesterday that Benny could run rings around you. I'm merely—"

She shook her head resolutely, her eyes closed. "If I lose this contest, it will be fair and square," she insisted. "I'm not going to sneak around making deals. We've gotten in this far, we may as well—"

"Yoo-hoo!" Britt called in. "The clock is running, you two. What are you waiting for?"

The crowd was just as impatient as they burst into a chant calling out her name.

"Angie, Angie, Angie—" It became incessant, drowning out any chance for more conversation.

Angie and Kyle took one last defiant look at each other. "You asked for it!" he cried. Without a backward glance, he raced for her house, making the crowd roar with excitement.

"Samantha?" Angie hollered. Samantha was already there, ready and waiting for her. "Run back over to our house," she ordered tersely. "Get anything that stains or sticks. See if we have any oil or grease."

Samantha dashed off as fast as she had come, and Angie headed quickly into the kitchen and checked the contents of Kyle's refrigerator. It was conventionally stocked as a result of yesterday's shopping trip, and she lost no time in choosing a bottle of ketchup, a full carton of eggs, and a jar of honey. It felt odd at first, deliberately making chaos out of an orderly house, but she quickly got the hang of it. By the time Samantha returned with motor oil and finger paints, the kitchen was a glorious mess.

"You should see what Kyle's doing to our kitchen," Samantha remarked fearfully, but there was no time for talk.

"Get that motor oil onto the floors," Angie ordered without missing a beat. "Benny won't be able to get any traction."

Samantha's eyes lit up. "Very clever, Mom. I'll dump some honey right by the front door so he'll get stuck the minute he comes in."

Angie's eyes gleamed as she made a trail of ketchup up the stairs. This was getting to be fun. It felt a little like a prank at summer camp, but what the heck, she figured recklessly. She could be just as juvenile as the next person when the occasion demanded it.

Samantha raced upstairs, carefully avoiding the ketchup, and proceeded to decorate the walls of the bedroom with finger paint. "Excellent," Angie commented briskly

Anything Goes

as she surveyed her daughter's handiwork.

"This is fun, Mom. Should I do the other one?"

"Be my guest." Angie laughed, but her laugh was short-lived as she stopped to imagine what was going on next door. Oh, well, it was too late now.

Samantha came running out of the bedroom laughing devilishly. She held up a multicolored hand for her mother to examine. "I left handprints all over the walls," she announced. But time was running out.

"To the bathroom!" Angie cried.

When they were done, the mirrors were painted black, the walls were smeared with Magic Marker, and for added measure, Angie poured a whole box of laundry detergent into the tub and turned the water on full force after stopping up the drain.

"Floods are coming," she announced as the water slowly edged over the tub and onto the floor. They watched as a deluge of soap bubbles began to make its way through the hall and down the stairs.

"It's like a bubble volcano," Samantha noted in wonder.

"Time's almost up!" Britt called through the loudspeaker.

Angie raced for the front door, and while the crowd cheered wildly and Britt counted down the final seconds, she took the finger paints and drew a huge picture of concentric circles. With the Magic Marker, she wrote: "This is not Kenneth Noland. It's what I think of Benny."

"Time's up!" Britt announced. "Everyone switch houses!"

Kyle appeared with Benny rolling along next to him. His hands were full of soot and his face was dirty, but he was still sporting his careless grin.

"Hey, Angie!" he called in a friendly manner. "I didn't know you had a tube of liquid glue in your house. That stuff is incredible!" He chuckled evilly. "Well," he said, "I have the distinct feeling you're about to spend the next nine hours cleaning. It will be a miracle if you get it all done." He laughed again. "As a matter of fact, it will be a miracle if you can even get into your house." He held up the empty tube of glue, still chuckling. "A miracle," he repeated, and headed in to see her handiwork.

Angie and Samantha walked across the lawn to their house and tried to turn the doorknob. It wouldn't turn.

"It's glued shut," Angie announced.

"Remember," Britt reminded her. "You must be ready by six. Good luck."

The knob didn't turn, but Angie wasn't fazed. With a simple credit card slipped through the crack, she was able to push open the latch. "Thank you, Mike Hammer," she said aloud, remembering how the famous television detective had picked locks. But once she got inside, she saw that that was only the beginning. Kyle had done unto her what she had done unto him, but worse.

"He went crazy with that glue!" she whispered, stunned.

Sure enough, hanging like stalactites from a cave ceiling were all her pots and pans, stuck together like upside-down pillars. She was able to pull them down, but part of the ceiling paint came with them.

Repainting the ceiling took fifteen minutes and vacuuming the soot from the carpets was tedious, but the glue stains on the walls were another matter. "Thank goodness for helpful hints," Angie said to Samantha as she got out the hair spray. A thorough dousing on the walls, and the glue was wiped away. She was beginning to feel better. Ernie the judge walked in and skulked around, making cryptic notes on a pad and nodding every so often. She didn't care. Let him write what he wanted. She could only do her best.

A couple of lipstick stains on the seats of the upholstered chairs were hopeless, at least for now. After a moment's thought, Angie decided to chance it and simply turn the cushions over. If the object was to cope in an emergency, she had certainly performed up to par.

After she had removed all the nail polish from the mirrors and vacuumed the coffee grinds from the bathtub, she looked around and sighed with relief. This wasn't so bad after all.

But her good spirits were dampened when she opened the closet door. Kyle had carelessly squirted mustard over the towels and sheets, and the sight of it enraged her. "Samantha!" she yelled.

Her daughter bounded in glumly, smelling vaguely of chocolate. "There's chocolate syrup all over the dining room. And did you see the spaghetti on the ceiling?"

"I must have missed that while I was working on the glue," she muttered. "That man has no limits!" She knew in the back of her mind that her own performance had been equally repellent, but she was in no mood to empathize.

"That's not all," Samantha said darkly. "When I put the dishes in the dishwasher, it started bubbling all over the place."

"Bubbling!" Angie made a face. "That idiot probably put dishwashing detergent in the machine. Did you at least turn it off?"

Samantha shook her head, chastened, and Angie raced

down the stairs to get to it. She was too late. The entire kitchen floor was awash with foamy bubbles, slowly spreading across the room like a live thing. Angie shrieked and kicked off her shoes, wading through the mess to turn the machine off.

"Here's the culprit," she said, holding up what had been a full bottle of detergent. "He dumped in the whole damn bottle."

"Come on, Mom," Samantha said, trying to cheer her up. "It's only one o'clock. I'll do all the laundry, and you do the bubbles, okay?"

Angie groaned as Samantha bounded off, leaving her to master the kitchen. She was still wrestling with the mass of bubbles when Kyle strolled in to have a look. She expected him to laugh, but she was wrong. He actually looked as harried as she felt.

"Mind if I sit down and join you?" he asked. Not waiting for an invitation, he plunked down next to her on the soapy floor. "I just finished getting up the last of that motor oil. Benny had a heck of a time in that house. I never saw him so frustrated before."

"What did he do, burn out a circuit?"

"Not quite," Kyle said. "He just had trouble plowing through all the soap bubbles from the tub. Quite a flood we had. Benny handled it, though. It took him a whole ten minutes, but he got it done."

When Angie heard that, she almost screamed. *"Ten?* That's all? Ten minutes?"

"We're practically finished," he added. "Oh, and the next time you use finger paints, make sure they're not soluble. A wet sponge took care of your daughter's artwork."

"Figures." Angie sighed. "What else is new?"

"Well, what did you expect?" He looked around. "It

looks as though you've got things under control here."

Angie threw him an ironic look that left no doubt as to her feelings about the day's events. "Is that so? This is your idea of control?"

Kyle leaned back against a cabinet and sighed. "Well, it hasn't exactly been a tea party for me either." He held up the control box and pressed one of the buttons. "I had to be on top of Benny all day. He's not programmed for this kind of cleaning, you know."

Angie was totally unsympathetic. "Poor you."

"It wasn't easy," he insisted. "There have got to be better ways to spend one's time."

"That's for sure," she said emphatically. "After this contest is over, I may be ending my career as a Supermom."

"Oh?" His eyebrow arched. "Why is that?"

Angie sighed in frustration. The man must be dense—or else oblivious to her needs. "You don't seem to understand, Kyle. My reputation will be ruined."

"Angie..." He turned to her and took her hand. "Don't you think you're taking this too seriously?" She didn't answer, and he lifted her chin so that she was facing him. "Come on, now. It's only a contest." She looked totally unconvinced, and he gestured toward the street. "You see all those people out there? They're your fans. They're not going to desert you. They'll still love you and they'll support you more than ever."

She saw the sincerity in his blue eyes and wanted to cry. But too much was at stake, and it wasn't over yet. "I wish I could believe that," she said dispiritedly.

"Besides," he went on, squeezing her hand, "you could take this as a marvelous opportunity to do things you never had a chance to do before."

"Like what?" she asked, somewhat suspicious.

"Oh, I don't know," he teased. "You could study modern art."

"Very funny."

"No, really, there's a lot you could do. You're a clever and talented woman, Angie. Does your column really take that much of your time? Think of all the other hours in the day. You could start a whole new business."

Angie's face fell. This was not what she had wanted to hear. "There are other alternatives," she said quietly. "Or don't those occur to you? Not everything is work, work, work, Kyle."

"Well, I know that," he began defensively, but she cut him off.

"Do you? I'm not so sure. If that phone rang right now and you had a meeting in Timbuktu, I think you'd go running off to it without a second thought." She looked down, knowing she was creating a sour mood, but she couldn't help it. It was true.

Kyle stiffened next to her, and she could tell she had gotten to him. But his next words surprised her profoundly. "I know it looks that way," he began. "But it's all I've ever known how to do. Call me an overachiever," he added, mustering a weak smile. "You won't be the first. I've always been so busy achieving that I never stopped to think about anything else. There was never anything better to think about. Until now," he added in a low voice, so low that she almost didn't catch it. "I've learned a lot from you, Angie."

"Me?" she gasped. "Oh, come on, Kyle. You're the brainy one. What could you have learned from me in this short time?"

"The difference between a house and a home," he answered at once. "The difference between a home and a laboratory. The realization that I've been on one fast track my whole life, and all other roads have eluded me. I always thought that was good—until you turned me upside down."

"Mom!" Samantha called from downstairs. "What kind of soap should I use on the mustard?" Angie knew that she and Kyle were on the brink of something very important, but she sensed that it might be too soon to pursue all of it now. Kyle was only beginning to open up to her, and she would do nothing to damage the true intimacy that was blossoming between them. She sighed and stood up. As deeply reluctant as she was to end this conversation, the contest was still looming over their heads like an ominous ghost.

"Come on," she said, offering Kyle a hand. "Let's go."

She got up and went down the stairs, Kyle following close behind. "Hand me that bottle of Wisk," she said to him, after looking at the towels.

He put his control box on the dryer and lifted up a few towels, parodying a detergent commercial. "Here we have an ordinary housewife with a laundry problem," he intoned.

"Knock it off, Bennett," she said, jabbing him in the ribs. She tossed the towels into the washing machine and started it up.

"What's next, Mom?" Samantha asked eagerly, still geared for action.

"Check the sheets in the dryer and see if they're ready to come out." She took a throw rug that was drip-drying on a clothes line and put it on Samantha's arms. "Put this in the dryer next."

"Aye, aye, Mom." Samantha saluted smartly. "Then

I'll go upstairs and get the rest of the towels, okay?"

Angie gave her a harried wave and marched back up to the avalanche of bubbles in the kitchen, Kyle still trailing behind. "Ugh," she said. "You'd think bubbles would just disappear after a while, as they do in a tub. But these are indestructible."

She was about to take a mop to the whole mess when she felt Kyle's arms around her waist. Taking her completely by surprise, he sat her down on the floor until they were lightly coated with bubbles.

"Kyle," Angie protested weakly. "How is this going to look? You're the enemy right now, you know."

"Don't worry, no one can see us through these bubbles. They're like a fortress. Besides, you didn't think I was the enemy last night."

He leaned over and kissed her with sudden, piercing sweetness. She was so drained and anxious, both from the contest and from her budding love for him, that she was almost ready to succumb, when a strange banging sound emanated from the basement.

"What's that noise?" she asked, but Kyle was too intent on kissing her to be concerned.

"Who cares?" he whispered ardently.

She settled back into his arms and allowed herself a moment of sedentary bliss.

"Even we homemakers need a little recreation sometimes," Kyle said as he pushed some of the bubbles from her hair. He kissed her again, and she wished fervently that the contest would vanish into oblivion. Her eyes closed to block out the real world, but the persistent banging continued relentlessly until even Kyle was compelled to open his eyes and listen.

"Sounds like a kettle drum with terrible rhythm," he joked.

Angie wasn't amused. "I'll bet Samantha overloaded the dryer."

"With what?" Kyle asked. "A tin can?"

Angie grew more worried. She looked at him for a moment, still listening intently, and impatiently pushed some bubbles from her face. The noise was too obvious to ignore. Samantha started coming up the stairs, and Angie immediately jumped up as her daughter emerged. The banging was still a constant boom.

"Be careful, Samantha," Angie warned. "I don't like the sound of that."

"I'll just turn off the dryer," Samantha said, and skipped back down the stairs, prompting Kyle to take Angie in his arms again. He was just about to kiss her when Samantha's harried voice broke into their exchange.

"Mom! Come quick. I can't stop the dryer. It's starting to smoke."

In a flash, Angie pushed away from Kyle and headed for the basement, taking the steps two at a time.

"Whatever it is," she said as she got to the bottom of the stairs, "it's going to destroy my towels."

Samantha was waiting in confused agitation.

"What did you do?" Angie asked her daughter above the banging noise.

Samantha shrugged. "I didn't do anything," she said guiltily. "It just started making that noise, and now I can't get the door open."

"Sounds like your dryer eats metal," Kyle said with a chuckle, but his laughter faded suddenly. "Hey," he noticed, looking around in concern, "where's my control box?" He ran over to the dryer as the something inside continued banging.

"Wasn't it on top of the dryer?" Angie asked, and then looked ominously at the dryer. "Oh, no."

Samantha looked more guilty than ever as Kyle stared aghast at the machine. "I must have knocked it into the dryer by mistake," she said, recoiling in shock.

Kyle made a dash for the dryer and futilely tried the door. "Pull the plug," he commanded. "Fast."

With one swift yank, Angie pulled out the cord, and the dryer stopped dead.

Kyle quickly pried open the door and reached in, gently retrieving the box. Although slightly dented in places, it didn't seem to be the worse for wear. He examined it for a second and then his mouth fell wide open in shock. "Oh, my God," he moaned.

"I'm sorry, Kyle," Samantha said miserably. "I really am."

"What is it?" Angie asked anxiously, seeing Kyle's distress. "What's the matter?"

"The red switch was thrown. It means that Benny could be totally out of control..." He let the last word drift off as a new and horrendous thought occurred. *"Benny!"* Suddenly hit by lightning, he bolted for the stairs, leaping up them four at a time.

Angie and Samantha exchanged startled glances as they heard Kyle run through the kitchen side door and over to his house. There was a strange silence that lasted all of twenty seconds, and then, like a thundering volcano, Kyle's voice could be heard shouting at the top of his lungs.

"AAAAAAGGGGGHHHHHHHHHH!!!"

Angie and Samantha traded one more glance and then bolted up the stairs simultaneously, heading for Kyle's house.

Reporters who had been lounging around all day made a beeline in back of them until they were all inside Kyle's

Anything Goes 163

living room. What they saw was unbelievable.

The entire place was in shambles. Furniture had been ripped to shreds and then turned upside down. The carpet had been torn from its foundation, the walls had gashing holes in them, and there were pieces of shattered glass from the broken lamps and light bulbs strewn over the floor. Angie ventured fearfully into the kitchen, where Benny was supposed to be preparing the dinner for ten. It was now dinner for no one.

"It looks like someone put a six-foot whirling blender in this kitchen and mixed the place into a huge purée," Angie noted as she examined the remains of a soufflé that was stuck on the walls in a complete circle as though the dish it had been cooking in had been swung around and around. It was still steaming from its own heat and looked like a peculiar piece of modern art. It appeared to be accompanied by all the spices from the empty spice rack, judging from the eclectic blend of aromas that surrounded it.

Stepping through mounds of food and broken plates, Angie gingerly picked up a dish from the counter to examine it. As she held it in her hand, it broke in two, the pieces crashing down along with the rest of the mess. Behind her, photographers and cameramen were snapping away. "What happened here?" Angie whispered, stunned.

"A tornado?" Samantha asked.

They continued their tour with utmost caution, as if expecting a monster to burst out of a closet.

"Spooky," a reporter commented in a hushed voice.

"Like a grade D monster movie, huh, Jim?"

"Get a load of the holes in the walls. Someone had a heck of an upper cut."

"That someone is a something," Kyle muttered as they all trouped into the upstairs bedroom. He sat heavily on what was left of the bed, totally dejected. Next to him was an utterly lifeless Benny, a ripped up sheet in two of his claws. A kitchen strainer decorated his metal head, and something resembling a bath mat was embedded in the joint of a metal arm.

Kyle held up the control box and shook his head. "The red switch was on, and every bounce in the dryer made Benny go berserk. This is the result."

Samantha's face crumbled and she began to cry. "I'm sorry," she wailed. "I'm so sorry." She ran over to Kyle and put her arms around him. "I'm sorry, I'm sorry, I'm sorry."

Kyle looked at Angie for a long moment. Then he knelt down and took Samantha in his arms.

"It's all right, sweetheart," he said quietly, kissing the top of her head. "Don't worry about it."

But Samantha wouldn't be consoled. Her tears continued to flow and she kept repeating her apology. Her slender arms went around Kyle's neck and stayed there. "It's not all right," she sobbed. "How can you ever forgive me?"

Her tears continued to flow, and Kyle looked at Angie with a new sense of rapport as he held her daughter in his arms. His arms tightened instinctively around the little girl, and something deep inside Angie opened up and began to crumble.

"The contest is over," Kyle said quietly over the top of Samantha's head. "I've lost."

"Oh, no, you haven't," Angie said, her voice trembling. Her heart contracted as she looked at them. "You haven't lost at all."

Chapter Eleven

"YOU WERE MAGNIFICENT, darling! Positively stunning." Britt Whittaker's gushing had absolutely no effect on Angie, who sat glumly staring at the lavish spread on her buffet. Samantha and Kyle were still sitting on the front steps, talking together in confidential, animated tones, and her eyes strayed curiously toward them as Britt rattled on.

"I *knew* you'd win," Britt was enthusing. "I had *complete* faith." She dipped a finger into the clam dip and tasted it. "Simply delicious," she pronounced. "Fit for a king."

Angie wondered if Britt would have said exactly the same thing to Kyle if he had won. "Uh, thank you," she said, trying to interject a rational note. "But I didn't win honestly." She tried to explain what had happened to Benny for the umpteenth time, but Britt didn't care. For the editor of *New Woman* magazine, this little publicity stunt was over. She was now planning a grand assault on all the TV networks, using Angie as the promotional gimmick.

"Not your fault the little tin can couldn't make the grade," Britt said dismissively. "Now, about that tour I've set up..."

"Sorry," Angie said, stealing another glance at her daughter and Kyle. "No tour."

"I thought we'd start in L.A. The Carson show wants to have you—"

"No," Angie repeated sternly. "I mean it, Britt. I've had enough."

But Britt Whittaker didn't know how to take no for an answer, and she wasn't about to begin now. "Oh, well, I guess you'll want a few days off to rest. That trip to Hawaii should give you a lift, though, shouldn't it? You'll get a *gorgeous* tan, which will be good for the TV lights and—"

"Forget it," Angie persisted. "I won't be going on any more tours. I've got a daughter to raise and—and ...besides, I've got other plans."

"Well, they can't be as good as what I've got cooked up for you."

Angie sighed. Britt was incorrigible. "How do I switch you off?" she asked as politely as she could. Her ears tried again to catch what Kyle was saying, but he was too far away.

Britt blinked. "Excuse me?"

"No tour," Angie repeated, mouthing her words distinctly. "For the last time. No more."

"But sweetie, *think* of the opportunities."

Something in Angie snapped. "Right now," she announced, "there's only one opportunity I need, and it's sitting out in front of this house."

She marched out the door and over to where Kyle and Samantha were sitting in the evening dusk. "May I see you a second?" she said bluntly to Kyle, crooking a finger at him. Samantha got up to join them, but Angie stopped her. "Alone, please."

After a reassuring pat on Samantha's head, Kyle joined Angie at a distance.

She took a deep breath and looked up at him, gathering all her courage together and praying that her boldness would work. "So, Bennett," she said bravely. "The contest is over. Now, what's it going to be?"

"Be?" He gave her that quizzical, highhanded look she had come to know so well.

She pressed on doggedly. "Between you and me, Kyle. Where do we go from here?" There. It was out. Inelegant, maybe, but to the point. Even if he walked away and she never saw him again, at least she had asked.

Kyle's face went through several rapid changes, reflecting his rush of emotions. At first it seemed that he didn't know what she meant, then he did, and then he hesitated, deciding what to tell her. When he finally spoke, it was with a gentleness that terrified her. She was positive he was about to "let her down easy." "Angie, look... I'm—I'm not... a normal person."

Her face flooded with relief. "Oh, I know that. We've been through that." She looked up into his blue eyes and thought about how true that was, and how much she loved him for it. It wasn't her fault if she had fallen in love with a hopeless eccentric.

"I can't cook, I can't clean house—heck," he added ruefully, "I can't even figure out how to operate the dials on a washing machine."

Her eyes twinkled. "Those aren't requirements.

Samantha can show you that. It's so easy that even a child can do it. I'm sure that with enough practice, you'd make a perfect homemaker."

"Hey, you two," Samantha called out. "Are you talking about me?"

"In a way," Angie answered slyly, but she wasn't looking at Samantha. She was still looking at Kyle. His face continued to war with itself, but she was growing more and more confident by the minute.

"Aren't you going to come in and have something to eat, Kyle?" she asked softly.

He shook his head. "I'm not hungry."

Samantha was stumped, for once in her life. She marched over to them and put her hands on her hips, frowning a little in annoyance. "What are you two talking about?" she demanded. "I think I have a right to know."

"You most certainly do not," Kyle answered her good-naturedly, "but maybe we'll tell you anyway."

He took Angie's hands in his and looked down at her. For the first time, she saw that the parade of reactions on his enigmatic face kept returning to a single, dominant feeling. Her heart swelled as she read the vulnerability and the brand-new evidence of love, so new that she was afraid to say anything lest it break like a bubble and disappear.

"I'm not very domestic," he began, as if daring her to contradict him.

"I know that," she acknowledged dryly.

"And I'm always working on some crazy project."

"True." She felt the beginnings of a smile teasing her mouth, but managed to keep a poker face.

"I'm really impossible to live with."

"You can say that again." The smile broke forth suddenly, a joyous smile filled with sunshine and hope. Kyle smiled back instantly, the mock antagonism replaced by the rush of love that was trembling underneath. "But I love every crazy bit of you," she finished, daring at last to say what had been building inside for so long.

"I've never been in love before, Angie," he said wondrously. "Not really. But you—you are the anchor I've always needed. Until I met you, I didn't know that I was on the fast lane headed for nowhere. You're like sunshine whenever you walk into a room. You make me never want to leave."

"What are you guys talking about?" Samantha asked, breaking into their reverie.

Angie looked down at her kindly. "Would you like Kyle to come and live with us, Samantha?"

Samantha's large brown eyes grew round. "Ohhh," she breathed knowingly. "I get it." An impish smile lit up her face. "Of course, I knew it all along."

Kyle and Angie both blinked. "You did?" they asked in unison.

"Of course," she answered loftily. "It was ineluctable."

"May I have your attention, everybody?" Britt's voice sang out above the din of all the guests. The house was swarming with photographers and friends alike as they all helped themselves to the spectacular food arranged on the buffet table.

Angie had cleverly and effectively chosen simple but impressive dishes that had not taxed her strength after the hectic events of the morning. Imported cheeses, caviar, and relishes served as hors d'oeuvres, a large and beautiful salad was arranged in a wooden bowl, and the marinated roast of veal sat on a board, waiting to be carved. A cold rice dish and string beans with cashews rounded out the meal, and peach melbas were being chilled in the refrigerator. Because she had prepared much of the dinner ahead of time, it had taken only an hour to put it all together. But she had taken the time to add lush bouquets of fresh flowers and candles in graceful holders, and had put up a colorful patchwork quilt on one of the barren walls, adding warmth and character to the room. She had had just enough time to shower and dress before the arrival of the judges and the guests.

Kyle, she knew, had not fared nearly as well. His dinner had been utterly ruined, and there had been no time to recoup. Benny had been put back under control, but Kyle's house was still a shambles, and the finale to the contest had clearly put him at a severe disadvantage. In the end, there was only one verdict the judges could reach.

But it wasn't a total loss. Benny *was* the hit of the party as he passed three sets of trays around to all the guests. Britt took a glass of champagne and raised it in the air.

"Attention, please." She pulled the puzzled contestants together and waved a photographer over to snap a picture. "I think these two have a little announcement they'd like to share with us," Britt said confidingly to the room full of people.

Kyle and Angie exchanged startled glances.

"I thought we agreed not to announce that here," she said to him, but Kyle looked just as amazed as she did.

"Don't look at me," he said. "I didn't tell her."

They both looked at once at Samantha, awaiting a confession, but none was forthcoming.

"Not this time," she mouthed from the sidelines.

"Well?" Britt coaxed. "How about it?" Angie and Kyle said nothing, and Britt evidently decided to take the bull by the horns. *"Well,"* she gushed, "it seems these two competitors are entering into a *new* kind of arrangement. If I'm not mistaken, they'll be sharing a nest before too long." She winked slyly and waited for the uprush of reaction she knew would come.

A ripple of surprise and curiosity spread through the group, mingled with spontaneous scattered applause. Cameras flashed as Angie began to back away, Kyle following her with a vaguely guilty look on his face.

"Don't look at me like that," Angie whispered to him. "You know something, don't you? Whom did you tell?"

"I did tell one person," Kyle admitted. "But he's not even here yet."

"Oh, yes, I am."

Angie turned and saw a wiry, nervous man standing near the door. He was dressed in a suit and tie that seemed to hang on his bony frame, and his hair was a mass of wild curls that gave him the appearance of an electric-shock victim. Angie had never seen so much raw energy bundled into one small person. He was carrying a bouquet of flowers in one hand and a bottle of champagne in the other.

Angie surmised that he could only be one person, and she walked forward calmly to greet him. "You must be Alpha, right?" she asked with a cordial smile.

"Right." The man handed her the flowers and turned to Kyle. "Congratulations, partner, we finally did it."

"We?" Angie asked. "You mean Kyle and me."

"I mean," Alpha bubbled on in his hyper way, "Kyle and me." He turned his vibrant grin on Kyle and waited patiently for his partner to get the message.

Kyle didn't get it at first, but suddenly, a metamorphosis took place on his face. "The contract," he breathed. "Alpha, you did it."

"For a hatful of dough," Alpha confirmed, holding up what appeared to be a contract.

Kyle grabbed it out of his hand and perused it avidly, like a condemned man who has just been granted a reprieve. He read the most crucial words aloud. "'Four KB 24 robots for the sum of one million dollars, of which fifty thousand will be payable on signing of this agreement...'" When he had finished scanning the document, he jumped up in the air with a victorious cry.

"We're in business!" Alpha said excitedly, slapping him on the back. "NASA wants two robots this year, and two more next year on its next shuttle flight."

Angie was totally perplexed. "I don't get it," she said. "One million for four Bennys?"

Kyle nodded ecstatically. "That's right."

"A million dollars," Angie repeated. "That's a quarter of a million apiece, right?"

Alpha popped open the champagne with a dramatic flourish and poured it too quickly into a glass so that it promptly overflowed. Undaunted, he toasted Angie, toasted Benny, and took a long sip. "Even with manufacturing costs we'll make a bundle."

Kyle's face was more animated than Angie had ever seen it. "To a new era," he said, raising his glass for another toast.

Angie remained stunned. "How can the average American family afford that?"

"They can't," Alpha said, oblivious to her concern. "Why should they?"

"Why should they?" Angie repeated incredulously. "Why, to replace the American homemaker with—that," she said, pointing to Benny as he rolled by.

Alpha explained, "Benny was not made for the purpose of saving the homemaker. Besides, you said it yourself, how many families could afford the price tag?"

Angie looked at Kyle, her face demanding an explanation.

"I needed the publicity," he answered readily. "Public awareness and all that. It was TV exposure that helped to promote Benny."

"Did you need this contest?"

"What I needed was two things. An excuse to move next door to you, and exposure for Benny. Benny gets the publicity, and I get you."

Angie wasn't sure if she was hearing right. "Then this whole contest was started because—because you just couldn't come right out and ask me for a date?"

"Uh, folks," Alpha broke in. "If I may interject here." He patted Kyle on the back and laughed. "Kyle was always on the shy side. *Very* shy," he stressed. He lifted one finger to make his next point. "But also very *sly*. Of course," he added, "not as sly as I am." He grinned at the two of them. "Oh, by the way... how was the opening at the Guggenheim?"

Angie's hand flew to her forehead. "The Noland tickets! So *you're* the culprit!"

"Hey, face facts here, people." Alpha held up his hands in protest. "You two set the stage. I merely rewrote the script." Kyle took Angie's hand and gave her a look so brimming with love that Alpha took the hint and faded into the crowd. They heard him saying something about the cute little woman with the reddish hair. "My kind of girl," he stated, making a beeline to where Britt was chatting vivaciously with the reporters. Angie and Kyle watched in fascination as Alpha put the moves on Britt, and they both laughed.

"You know something?" Kyle asked. "I think they'd go well together. Alpha has bizarre taste in everything—including women."

Angie took his arm and nodded thoughtfully. "You're right. Neither of them ever listens. All they do is talk, talk, talk. They may never hear each other, but they'll never know the difference."

They watched in amusement as Alpha guided Britt into a secluded corner, trapping her effectively as he leaned with one elbow on the wall in front of her. "Now that this contest is over..." Britt's voice wafted over to them, and they both groaned.

"She's got plans for me, but I'm not interested," Angie said. "This contest was enough for one lifetime. And it hardly seemed necessary. Honestly, Kyle. A million dollars for a bunch of Bennys?"

"Think of it on the bright side," he said, trying a positive approach. "The homemaker cannot be replaced for less than a quarter of a million dollars. Quite a price tag, wouldn't you say? Besides, what man wants to kiss a robot when he comes home at night?"

Angie laughed and felt a warm glow settle over her that she was sure didn't come from the champagne. A kind of happiness that she had never felt before was lighting her from within, giving her a sense of peace and security that she had never known before. She sensed that her joy was reflected on her face; she felt radiant. Kyle drew her close and kissed her gently, apparently indifferent to the fact that they were surrounded by people. Clearly, he was overwhelmed with his newfound happiness. As they were gazing at each other blissfully, Britt approached and congratulated them with surprising sincerity.

"If you really don't want to do the tour, Angie," she said, "why don't we wrap this up with an engagement party with full press coverage. I'm sure the readers will just *love* it."

Angie was quite surprised at this sudden turnabout, but she answered graciously. "Well, why not?" she conceded warmly. She was too happy to object. "How about it, Kyle? One more for the road?"

He nodded gamely, and Britt beamed.

"Good. And make certain that little robot person attends. He's a terror, but I know a good thing when I see it." Benny rolled by obligingly and Britt carefully took a glass of champagne and a Norwegian cracker spread with caviar off one of the trays. "Yes," she purred. "This little robot could easily replace the American butler. Easily," she repeated. She patted Benny's head and marched off to rejoin Alpha.

"Well, that's that," Angie said, bemused. "Who would have thought she'd give in so quickly?"

"She's in love with love," Kyle quipped. "And don't be surprised if she shows up on our honeymoon with a camera crew, especially since she knows where we're likely to go. I thought since the prize is a trip to Hawaii for two—"

Samantha dashed away from a reporter and interrupted them. "I heard you, Kyle. Does that mean I don't get to go?" she asked point blank.

"Not this trip," Angie said gently. "There are some times when Kyle and I are going to want to be alone, honey. But when we come back we'll plan another vacation and you'll be included, okay?"

"We'll be one big happy family," Kyle said enthusiastically. He wrapped his arms around the two new females in his life.

"Just the three of us," Angie added.

She felt a sudden pinch at the hem of her dress. When she looked down, Benny was tugging at her and making insistent beeping sounds. She put her arm around him with graceful resignation and laughed.

"Sorry, Benny," she said, patting his head. "I meant the four of us."

Second Chance at Love®

___ 0-425-08015-3	PROMISE ME RAINBOWS #257 Joan Lancaster	$2.25
___ 0-425-08016-1	RITES OF PASSION #258 Jacqueline Topaz	$2.25
___ 0-425-08017-X	ONE IN A MILLION #259 Lee Williams	$2.25
___ 0-425-08018-8	HEART OF GOLD #260 Liz Grady	$2.25
___ 0-425-08019-6	AT LONG LAST LOVE #261 Carole Buck	$2.25
___ 0-425-08150-8	EYE OF THE BEHOLDER #262 Kay Robbins	$2.25
___ 0-425-08151-6	GENTLEMAN AT HEART #263 Elissa Curry	$2.25
___ 0-425-08152-4	BY LOVE POSSESSED #264 Linda Barlow	$2.25
___ 0-425-08153-2	WILDFIRE #265 Kelly Adams	$2.25
___ 0-425-08154-0	PASSION'S DANCE #266 Lauren Fox	$2.25
___ 0-425-08155-9	VENETIAN SUNRISE #267 Kate Nevins	$2.25
___ 0-425-08199-0	THE STEELE TRAP #268 Betsy Osborne	$2.25
___ 0-425-08200-8	LOVE PLAY #269 Carole Buck	$2.25
___ 0-425-08201-6	CAN'T SAY NO #270 Jeanne Grant	$2.25
___ 0-425-08202-4	A LITTLE NIGHT MUSIC #271 Lee Williams	$2.25
___ 0-425-08203-2	A BIT OF DARING #272 Mary Haskell	$2.25
___ 0-425-08204-0	THIEF OF HEARTS #273 Jan Mathews	$2.25
___ 0-425-08284-9	MASTER TOUCH #274 Jasmine Craig	$2.25
___ 0-425-08285-7	NIGHT OF A THOUSAND STARS #275 Petra Diamond	$2.25
___ 0-425-08286-5	UNDERCOVER KISSES #276 Laine Allen	$2.25
___ 0-425-08287-3	MAN TROUBLE #277 Elizabeth Henry	$2.25
___ 0-425-08288-1	SUDDENLY THAT SUMMER #278 Jennifer Rose	$2.25
___ 0-425-08289-X	SWEET ENCHANTMENT #279 Diana Mars	$2.25
___ 0-425-08461-2	SUCH ROUGH SPLENDOR #280 Cinda Richards	$2.25
___ 0-425-08462-0	WINDFLAME #281 Sarah Crewe	$2.25
___ 0-425-08463-9	STORM AND STARLIGHT #282 Lauren Fox	$2.25
___ 0-425-08464-7	HEART OF THE HUNTER #283 Liz Grady	$2.25
___ 0-425-08465-5	LUCKY'S WOMAN #284 Delaney Devers	$2.25
___ 0-425-08466-3	PORTRAIT OF A LADY #285 Elizabeth N. Kary	$2.25
___ 0-425-08508-2	ANYTHING GOES #286 Diana Morgan	$2.25
___ 0-425-08509-0	SOPHISTICATED LADY #287 Elissa Curry	$2.25
___ 0-425-08510-4	THE PHOENIX HEART #288 Betsy Osborne	$2.25
___ 0-425-08511-2	FALLEN ANGEL #289 Carole Buck	$2.25
___ 0-425-08512-0	THE SWEETHEART TRUST #290 Hilary Cole	$2.25
___ 0-425-08513-9	DEAR HEART #291 Lee Williams	$2.25

Prices may be slightly higher in Canada.

Available at your local bookstore or return this form to:

SECOND CHANCE AT LOVE
Book Mailing Service
P.O. Box 690, Rockville Centre, NY 11571

Please send me the titles checked above. I enclose _____. Include 75¢ for postage and handling if one book is ordered; 25¢ per book for two or more not to exceed $1.75. California, Illinois, New York and Tennessee residents please add sales tax.

NAME _____

ADDRESS _____

CITY _____ STATE/ZIP _____

(allow six weeks for delivery)   SK-41b

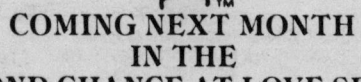

COMING NEXT MONTH IN THE SECOND CHANCE AT LOVE SERIES

SUNLIGHT AND SILVER #292 by Kelly Adams
Mississippi riverboat owner Noah Logan woos pilot Jacy Jones with laughter and understanding, lulling her with fond endearments and lazy days until he threatens to commandeer her life!

PINK SATIN #293 by Jeanne Grant
Voluptuous Greer Lothrop feels safer offering men chicken soup and sympathy than arousing their impassioned longings. But neighbor Ryan McCullough challenges her inhibitions and arouses shocking fantasies...

FORBIDDEN DREAM #294 by Karen Keast
Cade Sterling isn't merely Sarah Braden's former brother-in-law—he's a captivating male! Dare she defy social censure, her ex-husband's wrath, and secret guilt to fulfill their forbidden longing?

LOVE WITH A PROPER STRANGER #295 by Christa Merlin
Anya Meredith is utterly infatuated with stranger Brady Durant, but the mystery surrounding a silver music box... and disturbing incidents... suggest he's a conspirator in a sinister intrigue!

FORTUNE'S DARLING #296 by Frances Davies
Since winsome Andrew Wiswood, illustrious romance author, can't write when not in love, literary agent Joanna Simmons decides to seduce him herself, arousing him to prodigious feats of penmanship...and passion!

LUCKY IN LOVE #297 by Jacqueline Topaz
Opposing strait-laced Alex Greene on legalized gambling, devil-may-care Patti Lyon teases forth his more adventurous spirit, while he tries to seduce her into respectability!

QUESTIONNAIRE

1. How do you rate _____
   (please print TITLE)
   - ☐ excellent   ☐ good
   - ☐ very good   ☐ fair   ☐ poor

2. How likely are you to purchase another book in this series?
   - ☐ definitely would purchase
   - ☐ probably would purchase
   - ☐ probably would not purchase
   - ☐ definitely would not purchase

3. How likely are you to purchase another book by this author?
   - ☐ definitely would purchase
   - ☐ probably would purchase
   - ☐ probably would not purchase
   - ☐ definitely would not purchase

4. How does this book compare to books in other contemporary romance lines?
   - ☐ much better
   - ☐ better
   - ☐ about the same
   - ☐ not as good
   - ☐ definitely not as good

5. Why did you buy this book? (Check as many as apply)
   - ☐ I have read other SECOND CHANCE AT LOVE romances
   - ☐ friend's recommendation
   - ☐ bookseller's recommendation
   - ☐ art on the front cover
   - ☐ description of the plot on the back cover
   - ☐ book review I read
   - ☐ other _____
     _____
     _____

(Continued...)

6. Please list your three favorite contemporary romance lines.
   _____
   _____

7. Please list your favorite authors of contemporary romance lines.
   _____
   _____
   _____
   _____
   _____

8. How many SECOND CHANCE AT LOVE romances have you read? _____

9. How many series romances like SECOND CHANCE AT LOVE do you <u>read</u> each month? _____

10. How many series romances like SECOND CHANCE AT LOVE do you <u>buy</u> each month? _____

11. Mind telling your age?
    ☐ under 18
    ☐ 18 to 30
    ☐ 31 to 45
    ☐ over 45

☐ Please check if you'd like to receive our <u>free</u> SECOND CHANCE AT LOVE Newsletter.

We hope you'll share your other ideas about romances with us on an additional sheet and attach it securely to this questionnaire.

• •

Fill in your name and address below:
Name _____
Street Address _____
City _____ State _____ Zip _____

Please return this questionnaire to:
  SECOND CHANCE AT LOVE
  The Berkley Publishing Group
  200 Madison Avenue, New York, New York 10016